The Princess and the Peabodys

By
Betty G. Birney

SCHOLASTIC INC.
New York Toronto London Auckland Sydney
Mexico City New Delhi Hong Kong Buenos Aires

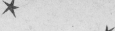

ISBN-13: 978-0-545-11004-4
ISBN-10: 0-545-11004-1

Text copyright © 2007 by Betty G. Birney. All rights reserved. Published by Scholastic Inc., 557 Broadway, New York, NY 10012, by arrangement with HarperCollins Children's Books, a division of HarperCollins Publishers. SCHOLASTIC and associated logos are trademarks and/or registered trademarks of Scholastic Inc.

12 11 10 9 8 7 6 5 4 3 2   8 9 10 11 12 13/0

Printed in the U.S.A.   40

First Scholastic printing, September 2008

Typography by Chloë Foglia

To the fairest of them all,

Remy Bella Frank

1.

Ye First Mistake

Once upon a time, in the magical land of Pine Glen, California, lived a girl named Casey Peabody— that's me. I still live in Pine Glen, and okay, it isn't *really* magical. At least it wasn't until the princess came—and then, the magic that happened was a lot different from what you read about in fairy tales.

The whole princess mess began on a typical Saturday morning for the Peabody family. And even if someone had told us what was coming, none of us would have believed it.

No reasonable person would.

"Remember: One man's trash is another man's trash," Dad muttered between sips of OJ that morning. My gran and I were gearing up to go yard-sale shopping, just as soon as we finished our breakfast, and Dad was teasing Gran about her passion for second-hand bargains.

"Listen, Joey." When Gran calls Dad "Joey," you know she's feeling feisty. "Some guy bought a painting for four dollars at a yard sale and guess what was behind it? An original Declaration of Independence. Sold for over eight million dollars. You can't call that trash!"

"You have my permission to sell anything in this house for eight million dollars," Dad said, bowing to Gran.

Duke, our shaggy English sheepdog, thumped his tail. "That includes you, dog," Dad added. Actually, I'm not sure we could get eight dollars for Duke. He has a major case of doggie breath.

Gran eyed the clock and I got the hint. "Ready to roll," I said with a yawn.

Duke, who insists on coming with Gran and me on our treasure hunts, pranced toward the front door and waited for us. Thankfully my little brother, Shane The Pain, doesn't care to tag along, so—not counting Duke—I have Gran all to myself when we go shopping.

"I've got a good feeling about this one," Gran said, checking her purse for her keys. "It's an estate sale at that big old house over on Drew Street."

"That monstrosity?" Dad asked as he poured himself some coffee. "Nobody's come out of there in thirty years."

Gran's eyes lit up. "My kind of house!"

Once we were on the road, Gran asked me about my homework situation for the weekend.

"Not too bad." I'd just finished my first week of eighth grade at Pine Glen Junior High. "They always take it easy in the beginning. After that they really load it on."

Gran turned the car onto Drew Street. "So school's okay so far?"

I shrugged my shoulders. "Same as ever. Girls like Eden Endicott still think they rule." Pine Glen was full of popularity queens like Eden. "But soccer is *awesome*," I added.

"Go, Panthers," Gran said with a grin.

"Go, Panther *girls*," I corrected her.

Gran eased on the brakes. There was already a traffic jam on Drew Street but she managed to find a small space and barely squeezed her station wagon into it.

"Everybody's out today." Gran said, amazed. "We'll have to move fast." She made sure to roll all the windows down halfway, and then she patted Duke affectionately. "The car's nice and cool today, Duke," she said, giving him a wink. "You stay here and we'll rush right back with our treasures."

As we walked down the street with the rest of the crowd, I realized how right Dad was about the creepy old Tudor-style house. The overgrown yard looked like something out of a scary movie.

"You take the linens over there." Gran waved her hand toward the open garage. "I'll check out the furniture."

I'm not the linen-and-lace type but Gran has trained me well. She even taught me how to elbow my way up to the table. As I reached for a vintage tablecloth with red polka dots, a tall woman with rhinestone-edged glasses snapped it up, along with several others. "*These* are mine," she announced.

I gritted my teeth and moved on to a stack of old-fashioned dresser scarves. The rhinestone lady tried to reach over my shoulder but she was too late. I quickly picked out the two best and put the rest down.

By the time I tracked down Gran, the yard was so packed with bargain hunters, you could hardly turn around.

"Find anything?"

Gran made a face. "Naw. Nothing left but junk. Real junk."

She *ooh*ed and *aah*ed at the pieces I picked out—
"good junk" she called it—and we rummaged around
a few more tables. Gran checked out a blue glass
pitcher. I went for some old magazines I found
stacked under a small, rusty metal box.

"Whoa!" The box weighed a ton when I tried to
pick it up.

"What's inside?" Gran asked.

I couldn't get the lid to budge. "Rusted shut," I
told her.

She tried shaking the box. "It sounds empty but
it's really heavy." She checked the tag on the bottom.
"The price is right. Let's take a chance. Maybe
there's something inside that will pay for your college tuition. Or at least a trip to Hawaii!"

Before we left, Gran settled up with the woman
running the sale. She even persuaded her to take a
dollar off the box's price on account of the rust.

Duke barked and wagged as we approached the
car. He knew what was next: hot chocolate and
chocolate-chip muffins at Herbert's Bakery. He
always managed to get a bite of muffin out of Gran
or me. I guess that's why he's such a fan of our
Saturday morning yard-sale trips.

As we slid our finds onto the backseat, Duke let
out a whimper.

"What's the matter, boy?" I asked.

He stared down at the box, backing away from it suspiciously.

"Scaredy cat," I scolded him. "What's the matter with you?"

"It's that old box," Gran said. "I don't think he approves."

As soon as she moved it to the front seat, Duke quieted down, but he kept his eyes fixed on our rusty prize.

"Dumb old dog," I said with a laugh.

I wish I'd paid more attention to him . . . because as it turns out, dumb old Duke was on to something.

2.

Ye First Meeting

As soon as we got home, Gran and I stashed our finds in her cottage. She has her own little house right in our backyard. When Mom died five years ago, Dad asked Gran to come live with us. He built her a blue cottage with white trim behind our big white house with blue trim. Roses and red geraniums surround the house. It's friendly and warm, like Gran is.

Gran plunked the linens down on a shelf, and asked me to lug the box back to the main house. Then I had to race over to school in time for my soccer team's afternoon scrimmage.

I turned down Gran's offer of a ride, preferring to

hop on my bike instead. Biking is my favorite way to warm up for practice, but on that day, it didn't do much good. Despite the two goals I scored, our side lost 3–2. My best friend, Alisha, and I worked off our frustration afterward, running three miles around the track.

I love running with Alisha. Her legs are inches longer than mine and it's a challenge to keep up with her. She's the only girl in Pine Glen who loves sports as much as I do and she does a *wicked* imitation of Coach Curson.

"Kick it, Peabody," she growled just like our soccer coach.

"I did kick it," I moaned. "What good did it do?"

"It's not whether you win or lose," Alisha said, slowing down to catch her breath. "Besides, you looked good."

"Yeah, but I'm worried about Carly. She's not cutting it as keeper. How many times did she trip over her own feet?"

"The keeper is *not* a 'keeper.'" Alisha giggled. "Maybe we should put a magic spell on her."

"It couldn't hurt," I agreed. I sprinted ahead and yelled back to her. "Come over tomorrow, okay?"

"Sounds like a plan," Alisha called back to me.

It wasn't until after dinner that Saturday night that I thought about the metal box again. I set it down in front of Dad and told him I wanted to test his strength.

He shuddered as he examined the rusty thing. "I don't want to touch that without getting a tetanus shot first. What is it?"

"One of Gran's bargains," I explained.

Dad gingerly picked up the box. "Whoa—heavy. What kind of metal is it?"

Duke tried to crawl under the sofa but he was too big to squeeze more than his head under it. We could still see his furry butt sticking out.

"What's up with him?" Shane asked.

"He's suffering from an incurable case of weirdness," I said. "Open it, Dad. You're big and strong."

He is, too. He manages his own construction company and does a lot of heavy lifting to help build houses.

There was no sound when Dad shook the box, so he tried to look through the tiny holes on top. "Nothing inside. But it sure has some heft to it."

"*Open* it, dear. Please," Gran urged him.

He grunted and made silly faces as he pulled the lid, then tried to twist it off. "Get me my screwdriver, Shane, will you? Maybe I can pry it off."

Dad ran the screwdriver under the edge of the lid but it still didn't budge. "This thing's been rusted shut for a long time."

Gran smiled. "Good! It really *is* old."

"It must have spent a few years in the rain," Dad said.

"Maybe it was buried in the ground," Shane suggested. "Like pirate treasure."

At eleven, Shane still hadn't outgrown his pirates-castles-and-wizards phase.

Dad put a thin coating of oil around the lid and tried twisting it off again. "Okay, I think . . . yeah, it's starting to loosen up!" he announced.

I got a tingly feeling at the back of my neck, like something important was about to happen. Duke whimpered softly.

"Shush, you silly dog," Shane said. "You're afraid of a box?"

"I think he's afraid of what's *inside*," I told him. I was starting to feel scared myself.

Then the box began to shake. Dad's eyes opened wide as it jiggled in his hand. "What the heck's going on?"

Bam! He dropped the box like a hot potato. The lid flew open and a brilliant golden light momentarily blinded me. I gasped—and so did everybody else. Duke's whimpering grew louder as a thick cloud of golden fog filled the room.

"Dad?" Shane's voice quivered.

"I'm here, son." Dad tried to comfort him.

Then an unfamiliar girl's voice cut through the fog. "Who is it that speaks? I command you to tell me at once!"

I was trembling as the fog began to dissolve. Little by little, I could make out the form of a girl, about my age, standing smack in the middle of our living room. We all stood around her, gawking like idiots.

From the first moment, I had no doubt that she was a princess, or at least somebody dressed up like one. With her long golden curls, sky-blue eyes, and creamy peach skin, she looked more like a storybook princess than one of the modern royals I've seen in magazines. They're usually dancing at clubs or sunbathing on the beach. This girl wore a long gown of pink satin with billowing blue brocade sleeves. Her entire dress was trimmed in gold braid. Pink pearl earrings adorned her tiny earlobes. But it was her crazy headgear that proved she was a princess: a glittering tiara, studded with what appeared to be real diamonds, rubies, emeralds, and blue stones. Sapphires, I guess.

"My, my!" Gran murmured. "It's a—" She didn't even try to finish her sentence.

"Dad?" Shane's voice was shaky.

Dad spread his arms out wide, as if to protect us. "It's okay. Everything's okay," he said, but he didn't sound convinced.

As the fog slowly faded away, the princess turned her big, beautiful eyes on us.

There was something rising up in my throat, something like a scream that was so big, I didn't dare let it out. Duke, however, didn't try to choke back his reaction. He gave out a huge, eerie howl.

"Dad!" Shane was in a complete panic now.

"It's all right," Gran said in an even voice. "Let's just all take a deep breath."

"Silence!" the strange girl cried out.

"Dad?" Shane asked. "This isn't happening, is it? She couldn't have been in the box, could she?"

"Of course not. It's just a . . ."

Suddenly, the princess clapped her hands over her eyes and screamed. "Oh, help! I shan't look! It hurts too much!"

"Maybe the light hurts her eyes," Gran suggested.

"Nay!" cried the girl, parting the fingers of her hands. "'Tis all too ugly! Your foul garments and this hideous chamber! Get you away! I must return to my castle posthaste."

Dad shifted uncomfortably and cleared his throat. "See here, miss, this is our house. And there's no castle around here."

The girl uncovered her eyes. "You call this a *house*? 'Tis a *hovel*!"

"Huh?" Shane asked.

"She means it's a dump," I explained.

"Silence!" shrieked the girl. Duke hugged the floor in fear and finally managed to disappear completely under the couch.

"Bow down! Bow down at once! I command it!"

Dad stepped forward. "Look, I don't know what kind of a joke this is or who's behind it." His voice was firmer now. "But we don't bow to anybody in this house."

"Bow at once or my father will behead you!"

"Is your dad in there, too?" Shane asked, nervously pointing at the rusty box.

"Bow! I command you!"

"For goodness' sakes, let's bow," said Gran. "Casey, curtsy, like this."

Gran attempted a wobbly curtsy. Mine was short and sweet, and Shane and Dad bowed sheepishly from their waists.

I guess it worked because little Miss Pretty in Pink calmed down, and Duke peeked out from under the slipcovers.

"'Tis better," said the princess. "Now, tell me, which road leads back to the castle?" She peered nervously toward the window.

"What castle are you looking for, dear?" Gran asked in her most helpful voice.

"Stupid peasants," she muttered. "*My* castle. Where I live with my father, your king."

"Who put you up to this? Casey?" Dad turned to me. "Is this some kind of school prank?"

Yeah, like the first week of eighth grade I learned how to make medieval princesses appear out of rusty boxes. That would be some science project. "Dad . . . I had nothing to do with it," I moaned.

"You'd better start from the beginning," Gran said. "Who are you and where are you from?"

The girl held her head high and adjusted her tiara. "I am Princess Eglantine Eleanor Annalisa Ambrosia de Bercy of the Kingdom of Trewellyn, daughter of Guilfoy the Great. And who, pray tell, art thou? The pigkeeper's family?"

Dad's jaw dropped. "Princess?"

Shane snickered. "Princess . . . Egg?"

I was just plain mad. "Pigkeepers!" With fists clenched, I was ready to teach this prissy snob a lesson. Luckily Gran stepped in.

"We're the Peabodys. This is Casey and here's Shane. This is Mr. Peabody and I am Casey and Shane's grandmother. You can call me Gran." Gran seemed to have a soothing effect on the girl. "I don't know how you got here, Princess, but you are in Pine Glen, California, in the United States of America. I'm afraid it's a long way from this . . . Trewellyn. I've never even heard of it." She turned to Dad. "Have you?"

Dad shook his head.

The princess bit her lip and looked a little frightened. For a second, I almost felt sorry for her . . . until she opened her mouth again.

"You are my royal subjects! Hence you will obey me! Now take me home anon. I command you!"

Dad scratched the back of his neck, the way he always does when he's trying to figure out the right thing to say. "Miss, we'd be happy to send you home if you'd tell us how to get you there. How do we get you back in the box?"

"And lock it so she'll never get out again," I whispered to Shane.

"Only Alaric knows the answer to that question," she replied.

"Who is this Alaric, dear?" Gran asked.

The princess stood up very straight. "None other than the royal wizard."

"Cool!" said The Pain.

Gran tried to coax the princess into sitting on the couch.

"If I am to sit, then you must kneel," the girl explained. "'Tis the law. And you must address me as 'Your Highness.'"

"Control freak," I muttered.

"Yeah," Shane agreed. "She's not *my* highness."

Once again, Gran took charge. "How did you end up in that box, Your Highness?"

The princess folded her hands and stared up at the ceiling thoughtfully.

"The last thing I remember 'twas my fourteenth birthday party. 'Twas most marvelous! There were bountiful gifts from throughout the kingdom. I received my weight in gold, this new tiara, and sweetmeats from the farthest realms of the earth. And my father, the king, gave me the most glorious music box."

She pointed to the rusty metal container. "It *was* most glorious until you urchins ruined it!"

I could feel my fists clenching again as the princess continued.

"Next, Alaric offered to perform feats of magic in my honor. My father, the king, commanded Alaric to make that box disappear and then reappear. Consequently Alaric waved his wand, said a few magic words, and . . . everything went dark!" The princess stopped and shivered. "'Tis all I recall!"

Dad stroked his chin. "He must have cast some kind of spell that put you in the box. He'd do that on purpose?"

The princess blinked. Hard. "Never. Alaric is like a brother to me. We have grown up together." She cleared her throat. "The trouble is . . . well, Alaric sometimes fails to achieve his goals."

"You mean he's a screwup?" Shane asked.

"Hush now," said Gran. "Go on, Your Highness."

"He is learning, but at times, he has been known to overreach," she admitted. "But this is really beyond the pale. To convey me hither to this wretched place!" She wrinkled her nose and sniffed. "It has an odor most foul!" She leaned over the edge of the couch and sniffed again.

"That's just Duke," Shane explained. "He needs a bath."

"Duke! The Duke of Olm was transported here with me?" Her eyes lit up. "Come out, you sprightly trickster! I command you!"

Duke sheepishly crawled out from under the couch.

"Poor Duke! Alaric has transformed you into a mangy old cur! Poor, poor Duke." She stroked his head. Duke whined dramatically.

This was too much for me. "That's our dog. He was here long before you showed up."

The princess ignored me. "At least I have one friend here," she murmured. Duke wagged his tail. The traitor.

"Let's not get distracted by the dog," Dad said. "Please finish your story."

"'Tis all I know," said the princess. "I shall have to wait until Alaric corrects his spell."

"How long will that take?" Dad's voice had an edge to it now.

"You never can tell," the princess replied. "In truth, Father deserves a more capable wizard. Especially after Alaric turned my lady-in-waiting into a big fat . . ."

Princess Eglantine never finished her sentence because at that very moment, the whole room began to shake and fill up with thick purple smoke.

3.

Ye Hocus Pocus

"Your Highness, I apologize for my tardiness."

When the purple smoke dissipated, it was unmistakable: Standing in the middle of our living room was a genuine medieval wizard. He wore the traditional pointed black hat—except it was tilted to one side—and long velvet robes that seemed a little big for him. In one hand, he held a black velvet sack— some kind of medieval backpack, I guess. In the other hand, he held a thick purple book with a shiny gold lock on the side. What didn't fit the fairy tale image was his face. There was no long, gray beard. In fact, he couldn't have been much older than I. Strands of wavy brown hair peeked out from under his hat, and he had the most dazzling green eyes I'd ever seen.

"It's a wizard! A real live wizard," Shane murmured in disbelief.

"*Tardiness?* Alaric, do you know how long I have been lost?" Princess Eglantine's voice was unbearably shrill.

Alaric seemed confused. "No. What day is it, Your Highness?"

The princess nodded toward my father. "Saturday" didn't make much of an impression, so Dad added the exact date with the month, and the year.

"Most astonishing," Alaric said. "Seven hundred years! Well, as we wizards say, 'time flies when you are . . .'" He scratched his head.

"Having fun?" Gran added helpfully.

"What? No, 'tis 'time flies when one is trying to break a spell.' Now let me see." He unclasped his book and thumbed through a few pages. "If I was able to transport myself here, 'tis a good sign, is it not?" Alaric didn't seem to notice that no one answered. Suddenly he smiled. "Yes, here 'tis. I shall return you to your birthday party in a flash."

"Only seven hundred years late," Dad quipped. "They've probably polished off the cake by now." Gran poked him in the ribs.

The wizard pulled a long silver wand out of his bag. It reminded me of the baton that Mr. Cooperman, the orchestra director, uses. Alaric waved it in the air just like Mr. Cooperman and began to chant. "Fiddia, liddia, kiddia, koo!"

I glanced at Shane, surprised that he wasn't even watching the wizard. Instead, he stared at Alaric's bag on the floor as several lizards, a frog, and a toad climbed out. Duke noticed, too, and began to bark.

"Squancy, dancy, fancy, doo!" On the last word, Alaric, his bag—even the amphibians and reptiles— simply disappeared. All that remained was a faint smell of cinnamon and ginger and a cloud of purple smoke.

Duke cocked his head to one side and whined.

"My!" said Gran.

"That wretched, wretched lout! He has done it again!"

The princess was still in our living room, and her cheeks were almost as purple as the cloud. "He has botched my departure again! Fool!"

Dad rubbed his chin thoughtfully. "Isn't he a little *young* to be a wizard?"

The princess sighed. "'Tis an unfortunate circumstance. Boricius was our wizard, a most ancient and well-practiced conjurer. He was the wizard of my grandfather and his father before him."

"That's old," said Dad.

The princess nodded. "When my father became the king, Boricius announced he was retiring to develop new spells. Alaric was a young orphan he had taken in and trained. So Father had no choice but to name Alaric our royal wizard, even though he is scarcely older than I am."

"Poor boy," Gran murmured.

"Alaric does a fine job with everyday spells," the princess continued. 'Tis just that this time, he . . ."

She never finished her sentence because—*poof!*—Alaric suddenly appeared again, along with more purple haze.

"Strange, 'tis it not? I seem to be able to move myself back and forth through time, but I cannot move you, Your Highness," he said. "'Tis a simple matter of adjusting the spell, of course. Now, let me see. Could you help me, lad?"

Shane's jaw dropped. "You mean . . . *me*? Help . . . *you*?"

"Yes, you shall do fine. If you would hold this book in front of me, perhaps I can do better."

"Not better, Alaric. *Perfectly*. Father must be royally furious!" the princess declared.

"Well, uh, not exactly, Your Highness. You see, directly after you disappeared, a messenger summoned him. He left the castle for Coothwaite."

The princess's shoulders slumped. "Not another war!"

"Do not begrudge him his pleasure, Your Highness. He does love a good battle," the wizard said, holding up his wand once more. "Now be a good lad and tilt the book up, thank you."

Shane took great care to hold the heavy book steady. I crossed my fingers that this time the spell would work.

Once Alaric repeated his hocus-pocus-mumbo-jumbo routine, he vanished again. Even the book disappeared from Shane's outstretched hands.

"Cool!" said Shane.

The princess did *not* disappear, and she wasn't any happier about it than I was.

"*Alaric! I command you to return anon!*" she bellowed. Her golden curls shook.

A few seconds later, Alaric dutifully appeared, mournfully shaking his head.

"A thousand apologies, my friends. Your Highness, I fear this problem requires more research. If your grace would remain here for a few days, I shall return with a proper spell. Good night."

With another puff of smoke, Alaric was gone before any of us could get a word in.

"A few days? Why, the last time he got the spell wrong he did not return for . . ."

"Seven centuries." Dad looked grim as he completed the princess's sentence.

We were all quiet for a while, even Her High and Mightiness. Then Shane finally spoke. "Didn't Einstein prove that time travel was possible? I think I read that somewhere."

"Where? In a comic book?" I mean, come on, he's *eleven*!

"It's getting late," said Gran.

I was amazed to see that it was almost midnight. With all the poofing in and out, I'd lost track of time.

"If Princess Eglantine is going to stay, we'd better make her comfortable." Gran turned to the princess. "Casey has an extra bed. You two can share her room."

I was shocked, but you should have seen the princess. She practically had smoke coming out of her ears.

"Nay, I shall not share a chamber with anyone! Especially a *boy*!"

"No, dear. This is Casey," Gran explained patiently, patting my shoulder.

The princess was unwavering. "He is wearing breeches. Only boys wear breeches!"

Shane giggled, but I was steamed. "I'm a girl," I said, taking off my baseball cap and pulling out the elastic band that held my ponytail. My dark brown hair fell to my shoulders. "Want me to prove it to you?"

Dad quickly stepped in. "I'm sure the princess is convinced. Maybe you can lend her some more comfortable clothes."

The princess jumped back, almost tripping over Duke. "Like *those* vile rags?"

"Don't worry. We'll find you something you'll like," said Gran. "Now, let's all go to bed."

"Must I share with her?" the princess whined.

"You'll like Casey's room. Trust me," Gran said soothingly.

My head was spinning. This wasn't happening! I was going to have to share my room with a princess who could out-princess the prissiest snobs at Pine Glen Junior High—no contest.

"Don't I have anything to say about this?" I asked, but no one seemed to hear me. No one else seemed to think that letting a princess move into our house was a royally big mistake!

"'Tis painfully bright in here," the princess complained, squinting her pretty blue eyes as she looked around my room.

"We've made some progress since the Dark Ages. Flick the switch and the lights go out." I turned off the light switch, plunging the room into total darkness.

The princess screamed. The wimp. I flicked the lights back on and she quickly covered her eyes. "Oh, too bright!"

"Like I said, that's progress."

I have twin beds in my room, which is great when Alisha sleeps over, but as I pointed the princess toward her bed, I wished Alaric would make it vanish. The princess sat down. Her tiara was crooked. Her dress was wrinkled. Her highness looked pretty low.

Gran entered with a frilly nightgown she'd found in her stash of yard-sale finds. "Here's a lovely gown, Your Highness. Before you change, I've put out towels so you can take a bath."

"Very well," Princess Egg agreed. "I will allow you to bathe me."

"I'll fill the tub. Then you can bathe yourself," Gran said sweetly.

They moved into the bathroom that connects with my room and Gran turned the faucets on. The princess, true to form, screamed. "Water is flooding the bathing chamber! We shall all drown!"

Gran turned the water off, then on again, to prove things were under control.

"But how will you heat it?" the princess asked. "It

takes hours to heat water for my royal ablutions!"

"It's already hot," I heard Gran say. "See the steam? Now just remember to take off your tiara before you wash your hair."

"I dare not remove my crown," the princess replied in a shocked voice.

"Just until you've finished," Gran told her. "I'll put it here on the sink where you can keep your eye on it."

Once the water was turned off, Gran came back into my room. Again, the princess shrieked. "Return at once, I command you! I cannot bathe alone!"

"I think you can handle it," Gran called through the door.

I heard the princess sniffle. "I have never bathed myself before," she whined.

Gran went back in but I could hear her say, "Here's the washcloth. Here's the soap. Undress and get in the water. Soap up the washcloth and clean every inch of your body. The shampoo is in the bottle—you wash your hair with it, then rinse it out. The towel is by the side of the tub. The gown is on the hook. Your crown is on the sink. We'll be waiting in here for you." Gran's voice was so soothing, I guess the princess couldn't complain.

"Poor thing," said Gran as she came back into my room. I'd slipped into the long baseball jersey I use as a nightshirt.

"Poor thing? She's mean and horrible!"

"She's afraid. Think how you'd feel if you were in her shoes."

"I wouldn't wear geeky slippers with gold buckles," I said. "And I'd be grateful there were people who wanted to help me."

I could hear Egg splashing around in the bathtub.

"She's going to feel a lot better when she's washed away a couple of centuries of dirt," said Gran with a grin. "That crown could use a good scrubbing, too."

Egg did seem calmer when she finally came out in the nightgown. Gran taught her to brush her teeth and finally tucked her into bed. Of course, she insisted on sleeping with her tiara on.

"Stay here, Your Gran-ness," the princess demanded. "I command you."

"I'll switch with you," I offered. I would have been more than happy to sleep in Gran's house.

"No, no, this is Casey's room," Gran explained. "You two girls belong here together."

Yeah, right. Gran had obviously lost it.

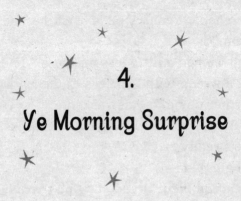

4.

Ye Morning Surprise

Surprisingly I slept soundly that night. And when I woke up the next morning, the spare bed was empty. My only hope was that the princess and her wizard had been nothing but a bad dream.

I tiptoed to the kitchen, where Shane stood before the open fridge. Dad was at the table, staring at Gran's rusty box.

"She's gone!" I announced gleefully.

"Naw. She's out in Gran's house," Shane explained. I knew it was too good to be true.

"The whole thing is impossible," Dad mumbled. "It couldn't have happened."

"Actually it could have." Shane reached for the

orange juice. "I looked up that Einstein thing on the Internet. It's hard to understand but he said mathematically time travel is possible. I think that Alaric guy is the real deal."

Dad sighed. "Yeah? Well, I wish he had a little more talent."

"I wish we had a little less princess," I added.

"What's wrong with Princess Eggle . . . Eggentile . . . what's her name?" Shane asked.

"I'll tell you what's wrong with Princess Egg," I said. "She's really *cracked*."

Shane giggled.

"She's *scrambled*," I added. "And that's no *yolk*."

"Maybe she's too *chicken* to go back home." Shane snorted at his own joke.

Gran bustled into the kitchen, dressed for the day. Following her was the princess, wearing Gran's pink robe and fuzzy pink slippers, and her tiara, of course.

"Say 'good morning' to her highness," Gran said brightly.

"Morning," we all mumbled.

"Arise and bow!" the princess ordered.

We didn't arise. Or bow.

"Anon! I command you," the princess said in a louder voice.

Gran intervened. "Dear, we don't have that custom here."

"We don't have any princesses in this country," Dad added.

"You have one now," said the princess. "You will adjust."

Dad had that look he gets when Shane or I mouth off. "*You* will adjust, young lady." His face turned red. "Now sit down and eat with the rest of us. *Anon!*"

Dad doesn't issue commands often, but when he does, people tend to obey. The princess sat down at the table without argument.

"I'm going to fix an extra-special breakfast," Gran announced, grabbing an apron from the pantry door.

"Pancakes!" Shane shouted.

"I second that," said Dad.

"Sausage?" I asked.

"The works," said Gran. "What do you usually have for breakfast, Princess Eglantine?"

"A joint of meat, a glass of wine, a loaf of bread," the princess replied.

"I'll have a glass of wine, too," Shane chimed in.

"We'll all start with orange juice," Gran insisted. "I'm sure the princess will like it even better."

Shane and I got up to help Gran, and to escape the princess's highly unpleasant glare. Dad picked up the newspaper and disappeared behind the front page.

"Did you check out the stove, Princess?" I asked.

"Instant fire. You do have fire in Trewellyn, don't you?"

"You're required to address me as 'Your Highness,'" she reminded me.

"Or what?" Shane asked innocently.

"She'll tell her daddy," Dad grumbled. "Then off with your head."

"Joseph!" Gran interrupted. "I taught you better about being a good host!"

Dad replied with a "Yes, ma'am," then turned to Egg. "Sorry, Your Highness."

The princess didn't seem to hear. She was deep in her own thoughts, and they were definitely not happy ones. It didn't seem like a good time to point out that her tiara was crooked. She took a sip of orange juice, then slammed the glass down. "'Tis *sour*! What 'tis it?"

"OJ. Orange juice. *Fruit* juice?" I tried to explain.

Dad cut in. "Do you think your friend the wizard will be back today, Your, uh, Highness?" Despite Dad's friendly tone, I could hear the tension in his voice.

"'Tis in his best interest," she said between clenched teeth. "We have always treated him like family, but he can be replaced."

Just then, the phone rang. The princess jumped up and screamed.

"Chill," I advised her.

"I'll get it." Dad headed to the den.

As the phone rang again, the princess stood there frozen, her mouth hanging open, her hand on her heart. "Are we under siege?" she asked.

"No, dear. It's the telephone." Gran gently guided her to the door leading to the den. Dad was saying, "Hi, Fred! Yeah, I did the specs yesterday. I'll fax them to you."

"He's talking to his business partner, Fred," Gran explained.

"Where is this Fred?" asked the princess, nervously looking around the room.

"He's not here. He's at his house," said Gran. "About five miles away."

The princess's eyes widened. "He is speaking to someone who is not here?"

"Yes, dear. Over the telephone."

The princess sighed. "The duke sometimes speaks to invisible beings as well. My father, the king, says 'tis harmless."

As Dad hung up the phone, Gran set a plate of sausages and pancakes in front of Princess Egg. "Pour her some milk, Casey," she instructed me.

"You possess a cow?"

I was too mesmerized by the force the princess used to spear her sausages to answer.

"Guess forks weren't invented in her day,"

Shane whispered loudly.

"'Tis my day *now*," the princess argued.

Suddenly there was a blinding flash of light. I jumped, sending a flood of milk across the table as purple clouds filled the room.

When the haze cleared, Alaric was sitting beside me as if he'd been invited to breakfast. He let his bag of goodies drop to the floor.

"Ever hear of knocking?" Dad asked him as he returned from the den.

"My deepest apologies. I realize my comings and goings are a bit . . . abrupt," the wizard replied with an apologetic smile.

"Would you like some breakfast?" Gran asked.

Alaric leaped up and bowed to her. "Fair lady, you are too, too kind!"

The princess rapped the table with her knife. "Really! You are not to stand whilst I am seated. 'Tis a simple rule."

"Would your dad really cut off our heads?" Shane asked.

The princess thought about it. "Were I to ask him to? Yes. Otherwise, he would merely toss you into a dank and dreary dungeon."

"Pancakes for you, Alaric?" Gran asked sweetly.

"You are standing! I am sitting!" the princess shrieked.

Dad threw his paper down and stood up, towering over Princess Egg. "Now listen, young lady. I won't have you being rude to my mother. It's not allowed."

"But I am your princess. . . ."

"Yeah. Well, this is my castle, and I am the king of this castle, so we go by my rules here. And you're dangerously close to getting thrown into *my* dungeon, which is right over there."

I was pretty amazed when Dad stomped across the kitchen and flung open the door to the basement. "There's a lock on this door, too."

"Pooh! You are not a king," said the princess.

"Perchance we could compromise a bit, Your Highness," Alaric suggested. "Remember when you traveled to Vandolia and you were forbidden to wear your jewels?"

"Nasty place with bugs as big as the duke," the princess recalled. Duke slinked under the table.

"My point is, when one travels to another land, one often adopts the customs of the place one is visiting," the wizard concluded.

"Perchance," the princess agreed. "However, if you were a competent wizard, I would not have to adapt to such primitive conditions."

My face felt really hot. "Primitive! You never even saw electricity or running water before yesterday. We're so *not* primitive. . . . Watch this!"

All eyes were on me as I stuffed a piece of bread in the toaster and rammed down the lever. It seemed to take a lot longer than usual, but when the toast finally popped up, to my delight, both Alaric and Egg gasped.

"My, that 'twas a most splendid spell," the wizard said. "Perhaps 'tis in my book?" He reached for his backpack.

Gran buttered the toast and served Alaric a slice. "Why don't we all finish eating first?" she suggested.

The wizard took a big bite and chewed slowly before responding. "Mmmm. Most delicious. Now, it seems we've come upon an unfortunate situation."

"What situation?" Dad asked.

Alaric swallowed hard. "The situation concerning the spell. 'Tis increasingly obvious that the spell I have been attempting possesses a flaw most annoying."

"The flaw being that it doesn't work?" Dad asked.

"Precisely."

The princess leaped to her feet. "But you are the royal wizard!"

"True," Alaric said. "I am not about to concede defeat, Your Highness. I merely need to conduct more, um, *research*."

Dad asked how long that would take.

"I would like to return to consult my grand master,

Boricius. Perchance he can help me undo what has been done." He looked over at the princess, who glared back at him. "That is, if you would care for her highness until I find a proper combination. . . ."

The princess stamped her foot. "Zounds!"

Alaric wiped his mouth with a napkin and grabbed his bag. "I have lingered too long here. Though I would like to learn the bread-toasting spell, I must go."

Within seconds, purple smoke clouded the room, then the wizard was gone, leaving behind the smell of cinnamon and ginger. *And* buttered toast.

I breathed in deeply. "Why does he always smell that way?" I thought for a second. "Like cookies."

"'Tis gingerbread," said the princess with a sigh. "Alaric simply cannot get enough sweets to satisfy him, and the royal cook indulges his sweet tooth by making him special batches of her famous gingerbread."

"Well, perhaps Alaric can bring me her recipe," Gran said wistfully.

"Perhaps. *If* he ever returns," the princess muttered.

5.

Ye Period of Adjustment

"I've got it the worst," Dad said that afternoon. "She called me 'Your Royal Dadness.'" Dad, Shane, and I were curled up on the family room couch discussing our princess problem.

"At least you don't have to share a room with her," I argued.

"What about poor Duke?" Dad countered. "She's been whispering in his ear all morning."

I sighed. "Lucky for him, he can't understand her."

Dad shook his head. "I stayed up late doing research, and I couldn't find anything that says this Trewellyn place even existed. I'm going to get some fresh air and try to clear my head."

Dad left Shane and me on the couch. Gran and her highness were out in Gran's little house trying to come up with clothes that Egg and the twenty–first century would both find acceptable.

"I wish the princess would leave poor Gran alone," I complained.

"I don't think she minds," Shane said. "You know Gran, she's always helping somebody."

I rubbed my eyes. "Well, Egg reminds me of the Wicked Witch of the West."

"I think she's kind of pretty," Shane said softly.

The Pain was really living up to his nickname.

"Pretty? All those awful things come out of her mouth, like 'Off with your head,' and you think she's pretty?"

Shane shrugged his shoulders. "Kind of."

A horrible thought occurred to me. "You don't *like* her, do you?" I asked in my most severe big-bad-sister tone of voice.

He shrugged. "She's not that bad."

I gave him a devastating glare, which sent him running toward the hallway.

"Outta here," he said, and then he was.

I punched a cushion and settled back to wonder how my brother could like the princess. It was just like Eden Endicott and her impossible posse of friends at school. Sure, they were pretty, but they'd just as soon throw you in a dungeon as smile at you, and still . . . they were popular. Everybody just went along with them. Especially the guys.

A moment later, Gran led Egg into the family room. I pretended to be really interested in the TV.

"Zounds!" the princess exclaimed. "What strange creatures abide in that box?"

It took me a few seconds to realize she was talking about the television set.

"It's where we keep our captives. It's even better than a dungeon." I pointed to the screen, where two boring reporters discussed the news.

The princess's peaches-and-cream skin turned dead white.

"'Tis people, only they are so tiny. Are they fairies?" she asked earnestly.

Gran stepped in, shaking her head. "Dear, it's just a device for entertainment. I don't think she's ready for this, Casey."

"Ready for what?" Dad walked in.

"Just think how much she could learn about contemporary culture from TV." I switched to the music channel where some goth girls were writhing and showing off their piercings.

"Oh! You have captured some peasants!" Egg exclaimed.

"Hold on there," Dad said. "That's more contemporary culture than we need right now." He flicked the remote until he found a football game.

Egg edged closer to the TV. "And what might that be?"

Dad settled down in his favorite chair. "Football. It's sort of like a joust. Sit down and I'll explain it to you, Your Highness."

Gran maintained her look of disapproval. "I don't think she's ready for football either," she said firmly. "And I still have to find her some clothes." She headed back to her house, just as Shane reappeared in the doorway. "Egg? I mean, Your Princessness? I have something cool to show you."

"*Cool?* Do I need my cloak?" Egg hurried to follow him.

I was totally disgusted. Egg had taken over our household. Gran was knocking herself out to please her, Shane thought she was pretty, and now Dad wanted to teach her the finer points of football. I didn't know exactly where Duke was, but I was sure he was somewhere near the princess.

I banished myself to my room for some peace and quiet and I tried to work on my algebra homework, but my mind kept wandering. I found myself thinking that there must be an equation that would send the princess back to Trewellyn forever. Then I heard loud noises coming from Shane's room, where I found Egg and The Pain sitting side by side in front of his computer.

"I have no understanding of how those small knights got in that box," said the princess, pointing at the screen. "Are you a wizard, Master Shane?"

"Sort of," The Pain bragged. I groaned.

"Let the joust begin!" a voice cried out. I'd only heard that line about a million times when Shane played his favorite computer game, Battle Royal.

The princess gasped. "How I love a good joust!"

"You've been to a real joust?" My brother was pretty excited.

"Who do you think awards the prizes? But it can be most messy. Father loses his best knights that way."

Shane pointed at the screen. "Okay, here's the castle."

"Duke!" the princess called loudly. "Duke, come see this castle!"

Duke jumped down from Shane's bed—where he's not supposed to be in the first place—and rushed to her side. I wanted to throw him *and* Shane into the dungeon.

"I'm supposed to find the Black Knight's chamber," The Pain explained. "Maybe you can help me."

"I shall try," said the princess.

I thought I might barf, so I was out of there. Not that anybody noticed.

I decided to get some juice and when I opened the refrigerator—*whoosh*—out poured a huge plume of purple smoke, then Alaric appeared before me. His lips had a bluish tinge and a piece of lettuce was stuck to his sleeve. He had a bowl of grapes in one hand.

"Ah, I am pleased to be released. I miscalculated my navigational points and ended up in that icy chamber. *Brrr*. Cold as the dungeon in the dead of winter! Thank you, fair lady."

I'm nobody's fair lady, but I let it slide. "How long were you in there?"

The wizard stroked his chin. "Time is not my strong point." As if I hadn't noticed. "By the way, the grapes are most excellent, ripe, sweet, and juicy." I guess time travel makes a guy hungry because Alaric was really chowing down. "Where is Princess Eglantine?" he asked with his mouth full.

Was that all anybody could talk about—*the princess*? I sighed and pointed in the general direction of Shane's room. "Just follow the noise," I said. Then I took a swig of juice from the carton in the fridge and headed out back to see Gran.

Gran was fussing over bits of lace out in her house when I arrived.

"I'm glad you're here," she said. "I'm having a hard time convincing Eglantine that the clothes she wants to wear would attract too much attention on the street."

"On the *street*? You're not going to let her be seen outside the house, are you?" It was the worst idea I'd heard yet.

"Casey, honey, she can't be locked up like a prisoner," Gran explained.

"Why not? Like Dad says, the basement makes a perfectly good dungeon."

"Casey." Gran sounded disappointed in me.

"Okay. She can come out on Halloween."

Gran stared at me over the top of her glasses. "What if you ended up in her time and place? I'd want someone to help you."

"Her father would probably put me in the dungeon."

"I think it would be fun to visit Trewellyn," said Gran. "I'd especially like to meet the duke!"

I burst out laughing. "He probably has shaggy hair, big ears, and bad breath."

It felt good to laugh with Gran. We hadn't had

much to laugh about since the princess arrived.

"The wizard wouldn't look too bad if he got some new clothes," I said. "Oops, I almost forgot. He's back again—in Shane's room."

"Maybe all our problems will soon be over, then," Gran said.

"Yeah. He'll probably make Shane disappear and leave the princess here."

Gran jumped up. *"What a terrible thought! We better go check."*

She dashed out and I followed, but I wasn't worried. After all, if Shane disappeared, the princess could have his room.

6.
Ye Hiding and Seeking

Gran looked really relieved to see Shane and the princess staring at Shane's computer screen.

"Is Alaric here?" Gran asked.

"Was. He's trying to reach that Boricius guy to help him," Shane said without taking his eyes off Battle Royal.

"What's that?" he asked the princess, pointing to something on the screen.

"That would be the barbican. Our castle has a much bigger one, doesn't it, Duke?" Egg proudly explained.

I'd totally forgotten that I'd invited Alisha over until a moment later when the doorbell rang. I made sure I got to the door first.

I eased myself out onto the front porch, closing the door behind me. The last thing I needed to do was explain the princess to Alisha. "What's up?" I asked casually.

"You invited me over, remember? Anyway, let's walk down to the Pizza Palace. There's a bunch of kids meeting down there."

"What kids?"

"Lindsey, Tino, Noah, Maddy. Lots of people," she explained.

"Is Taj going to be there?" I hated the tone in my voice but I knew which person Alisha was *most* interested in.

"I don't know." She tried to sound offhanded about it. "He might be there."

"Ah—I'm going to stay home and watch some soccer videos instead, pick up some tips," I lied. I crossed my fingers, hoping she wouldn't say she'd join me. I just wanted to keep her (and everyone else) as far away from Princess Eglantine as possible.

Alisha frowned. "Lighten up! I love soccer, but I don't mind having a little fun once in a while."

"I don't consider the scene at the Pizza Palace *fun.*" Especially not if I had to sit there alone while Alisha flirted with Taj.

"How would you know, Casey? You've never been there. And don't tell me you don't like guys. You told me you'd go to the ends of the earth for David Beckham."

"I don't think *he'll* be at the Pizza Palace," I said.

Alisha sighed. "What's up with you? It's just a slice of pizza. I'm going down there."

She headed down the sidewalk but stopped and turned back. "I really wish you'd come. I hate to go down there alone."

Ouch. She sure knew how to make me feel guilty. But the idea of talking to guys at the Pizza Palace made me want to run in the other direction. What if a boy talked to me and I didn't know what to say? What if a boy I didn't like talked to me? Actually I could probably count on the worst case scenario: No boys would talk to me at all. But today, I might have gone with Alisha . . . if it hadn't been for the princess.

"Maybe some other time." I didn't sound convincing.

Alisha shrugged. I could tell I had disappointed her, but I just stood there feeling like a jerk as my best friend hurried away.

After Alisha left, I decided to take my own advice and work on my soccer skills. Dad had used the garage wall, which had no windows, to chalk a large grid for me. I could practice my control by aiming and kicking the ball at different squares. It felt good to let off steam. I kicked that ball like I'd never kicked it before. Once for the princess. Once for the stupid wizard who started this mess. Then I gave it a good solid kick for me missing out on the Pizza Palace. It was a big kick that unfortunately bounced off the corner of the garage and sailed straight toward Gran's window. I watched it shatter the glass, as if it were happening in slow motion.

Gran rushed out, of course. "Casey! You scared the daylights out of me."

"I'm sorry, Gran. I can't do anything right today."

"It's not the end of the world. Come help me clean up the glass." She put her arm around my shoulder and I didn't pull away.

"See . . . it's all her fault. I was thinking about the princess and now this! How long do we have to keep her?"

"Keep her? She's not a dog."

"Well, can't we turn her in to the police? Or—I don't know—isn't there a home for obnoxious princesses?"

"I know it's a challenge, honey. But Eglantine's life has not been all maypoles and jolly jousts, either. She's been telling me all about it. Her mother succumbed to a bad draft in the castle a few years back. Her father is always involved in some war or another. And all the king's horses and all the ladies-in-waiting sound like a pretty poor substitute for a family. She's practically a prisoner in her father's castle, and all she's allowed to do is embroider. Plus she'll eventually be married off to some prince she's been engaged to since she was four. Sounds pretty dreadful."

"So . . . does she have to ruin my life, too?"

Gran didn't have a chance to answer because Duke started barking like crazy. "That's his 'company's coming' bark," Gran said, rising.

"Gran—we can't let anyone see Egg!"

Gran acted surprised. "Why not?"

"The tiara. The gown. Everything."

By the time we were back in the house, Dad was standing in the living room with Mrs. Huddleston from next door. Facing them were Shane and the princess.

"Yep, Egg, uh, Eglantine's a cousin. Visiting from England," he nervously explained.

"Well, welcome, Eggul . . . Eggla . . . uh, welcome to the U.S.A. My, you are a pretty girl!" Mrs. Huddleston looked the princess over. "You know, I thought folks in England dressed like us nowadays."

"I am a princess," Egg announced.

"That's a good one!" Dad laughed a little too heartily, obviously realizing that his story was quickly falling apart. "Eglantine's going to one of those medieval fair things."

"It's a lovely costume," Mrs. Huddleston said. She spotted Gran. "Hi, Libby. Are you finished with this morning's paper? I'd love to steal the coupon insert if you aren't going to use it."

Mrs. Huddleston asked for our coupon insert every Sunday. She was too cheap to buy her own paper.

When she finally left, Gran cornered Dad. "I think we'd better get our stories straight. I told Dorothy the princess was an exchange student." Dorothy is our neighbor on the other side.

"I e-mailed my friends that a real princess was staying with us, but nobody believed me," Shane admitted.

"Okay, we need a game plan," Dad said. "Come on, sit down, everybody. You too, Princess."

"And the duke?" Egg asked.

"Duke's always welcome," Gran replied.

We all sat down. "You understand, Princess," Dad began, "that if we told people the truth about how you got here, they'd lock us up."

"In the dungeon?"

"Not exactly. What I mean is, they'd think we

were lying or funny in the head. We need to decide who you'll be," Dad continued. "Cousin from Europe? Exchange student?"

"Alien from another planet," I muttered.

"I like the cousin. From some little country, like Luxembourg," said Gran.

"Never. I am from Trewellyn," Egg replied.

Dad hesitated. "I hate to tell you, Princess. Trewellyn doesn't exist anymore."

The princess leaped up. "Off with your head!" she shouted.

"I'm sure it's still there, dear. It's just called something else," Gran said.

"Of course it exists. My father, the king, is fighting to defend it anon!"

"I'm sure he is, dear. But what we're getting at is, well, if Alaric isn't able to get you back home for a while, then you'll have to live a more modern life here," Gran explained. "You'll get used to our customs."

She didn't sound too convinced. I certainly wasn't.

Dad nodded. "I guess you'll have to go to school."

It was my turn to leap off the couch. "School? She can't go to school!" If I sounded hysterical, it's because I was.

"Sit down, Casey. There's no reason why she can't," said Gran.

"Well, she's not going to *my* school," I insisted. "Because nobody there wears a tiara or commands people to bow! She'll be a total outcast."

"That's quite enough, young lady," Dad said. "Millions of people come here from other countries and they succeed. And they don't even know the language to start with."

"She says ''tis,'" I reminded him. "And 'perchance.'"

"I admit we have some obstacles here. Like no birth certificate. I can call Jack Talbot. I did that addition on his house last year—he'll work something out."

Mr. Talbot was our principal—this was getting serious.

"No way!" I burst out. But I changed my tone as soon as I saw the fire in Dad's eyes. "Dad, please. At least give Alaric time to *try* to get her back. And give us time to teach her the ropes. Otherwise they'll eat her alive."

That got the princess's attention. "Are there to be dragons at school?"

"It's just one of those funny expressions," Dad told her, all the while glaring at me. Then he turned to Gran.

"Mom?"

"I think Casey has a point, Joe," Gran said.

"Let's see what the week brings then," he agreed.

"May I say something?" asked the princess in an edgy voice. "In this country are people forced to do things they do not want to do?"

"They are if they're kids," Shane said.

"Since I am not a baby goat, might I make a petition?"

Dad nodded. "Petition away, Your Highness."

"I do not need to go to school because I am already the most highly educated female in my kingdom."

She waited for this to sink in, then continued. "All my life, I have studied under the tutelage of Boricius, the royal mathematician, my ladies-in-waiting, and my father, the king. I manage the royal household accounts, I embroider beautifully, I play the lute and sing, and I know how to read." She hesitated. "I can also juggle three apples, but do not tell my father, the king. He would not approve."

"Can you teach me to juggle?" Shane asked.

Gran cut The Pain off. "You are very accomplished, Your Highness. But school here is a bit different. You'll love it. You'll meet lots of people your own age—girls *and* boys. And you'll enjoy your classes much more than you'd enjoy sitting around the house with me."

"Boys?" The princess raised her eyebrows practically up to her tiara. "The boys in your country go to school with girls? Do they study the same things?"

"We don't take embroidery," Shane said.

"Do girls fight with lances?"

Dad laughed. "No, but I'm sure if they did, Casey would be at the top of her class."

"They study history, English, mathematics, music, and art," Gran explained.

"And P.E.," I added.

The princess frowned. "And P.E. 'tis . . . ?"

"Physical education. Sports. Exercise." I was feeling wicked. "Things that make you sweat."

"Zounds!"

"If she *does* go to school, she can't be called Princess," I insisted.

The princess shuddered. "Well, I shall not be called Egg."

"But you could be called Eglantine. After all, that's your name," Gran said firmly.

Dad cut off the discussion and went out to fix Gran's window. But my worries were just beginning. To be honest, I'd have rather faced a fire-breathing dragon head-on than walk down the halls of Pine Glen Junior High with the princess by my side. *That* was the kind of attention I could live without.

I could just imagine what Eden Endicott and her snob squad would think.

I couldn't possibly imagine what the boys would think.

Zounds, indeed!

7.

Ye Preparation

First thing Monday morning, I headed for Alisha's locker. I didn't blame her for pretending not to notice me.

"Alisha, I'm sorry. I was kind of stressed out yesterday and I acted . . . weird."

"Totally," she said without a trace of a smile.

"I've got a problem that's making me crazy. It's my cousin, Egg. She's staying with us."

Alisha stopped ignoring me. "You've got a cousin called *Egg*?"

"She's making me crazy. She's from this creepy country and she acts completely bizarre."

Alisha was still stuck on the name. "Is her

name really *Egg*?"

"It's Eglantine, okay? So what am I going to do?"

"Just how weird is she?"

"She's never been in a car before, she wears a tiara, and she thinks everybody has to obey her," I explained.

"Wow." I had Alisha's full attention.

"It gets worse," I continued. "Dad and Gran want her to come to school here. With me. With my luck, she'll be in all my classes."

Alisha slammed her locker door shut. "That could be trouble."

"No kidding," I agreed. "Hey, how was the Pizza Palace?"

"Fun!" She sounded as if she meant it. "You should come sometime."

I wasn't in the mood to argue with her again. "Okay," I answered. "Look—about yesterday—you forgive me?"

"Forgive you for what?" Alisha asked with a grin.

That's why I love Alisha.

When the bell for first period rang, I turned to make a mad dash down the hall and ran smack into Eden Endicott.

"Hey, watch it! You scuffed my shoe!" she whined. "My brand-new shoes," she added, turning to her ever-present entourage, Sabrina Toth and Kiki

Green, for sympathy.

"I'm sorry. I really am," I apologized.

"*I'm* sorry you're such a klutz," Eden snapped back.

Klutz? I'd like to see her score a game-winning goal in the last three seconds of a match.

"It was an accident," I explained.

Eden rolled her eyes and marched past me. "I hope that shirt was an accident, too!" she said with a nasty smirk.

"Yeah, I'd hate to think she wore it on purpose," Kiki added, giggling.

They all got a good laugh out of that one.

All through my classes that day, I had trouble concentrating. I kept picturing Egg with her long dress and a tiara sitting next to me. And I wasn't looking forward to the comments from Eden and her clique when they saw me with her.

When I got home after soccer practice, Gran greeted me with a big hug. "How was your day, dear?" she asked.

I shrugged. "Okay, I guess."

"Well, we made a lot of progress while you were at school," Gran explained. "The princess and I called your dad and she had her first phone conversation. We even took a ride in the car. It was a white-knuckler for her at first, but after a while, I think she enjoyed it."

"Great." I'm afraid I couldn't fake much enthusiasm.

"I think we made some progress in the wardrobe area, too. Come see."

Gran led me into the den where Egg was waiting. "It's quite original, I think," Gran said. "And it was all her idea."

Well, I *guess* you'd say Egg's outfit was original. For one thing, she was wearing some old curtains Gran picked up at a yard sale. Pink with blue flowers. Okay, she had actually made them into a short skirt but it didn't look like any skirt I'd seen at Pine Glen so far.

Over the skirt was a long pink tunic—a pullover with short sleeves. The tunic was cinched at the waist with a gold braided belt suspiciously similar to the tiebacks on our living room draperies. Her long, golden hair was held back by two barrettes decorated with colored stones. On her legs: criss-crossed blue ribbons. On her feet: pink ballet slippers. The princess seemed very pleased with herself.

"I am glad to see I do not have to wear breeches after all," she said.

"Gran, nobody dresses like that." I pointed to the princess.

"Why should I dress like anyone else? I am a princess." Egg held her chin high. "People expect me to be different."

"Well, they won't be disappointed." I headed straight for my room to hide while I still could.

For the next few days, I was highly motivated to get to school early and stay as late as possible, just to get away from the princess. I used the extra time in the morning to run and after school to practice soccer. I've always been competitive but I threw myself into my playing more than ever. At the end of practice on Wednesday, I heard Coach scream, "Peabody! Talk!" Her voice was almost as piercing as her whistle. And all the girls on the team knew that "talk" meant "trouble."

Coach patted the space next to her on the bench and I sat down. "Peabody, you know I have high hopes for you."

I waited for the "but." I didn't wait long.

"But . . . I thought you'd be more of a team player. You've proven you can score points, but you're missing chances to pass to teammates who have a better shot at the goal than you do. That's risky behavior.

It's not all about you out there."

I didn't know what to say. Maybe I didn't trust some of the other girls with the ball. Maybe I was trying too hard to be a star.

Coach must have read my mind. "Maybe you're a control freak. Maybe you're a ball hog. Either way, you've got to learn to let go. Or I'll be letting you go."

I think I gasped pretty loudly. "Give me another chance—please!"

Coach patted my arm. "Don't worry, we're not there yet. I just want you to work with your team-mates on the field. The more you help them, the more the team will benefit, you know?"

"I know," I answered.

I ran a couple of miles after practice, trying to get those words "I'll be letting you go" out of my head. It didn't work.

That night, Gran and the princess were out in Gran's cottage, sewing. It was too quiet in my room to concentrate, so I decided to visit Dad's home office. He was so intent on the computer that when I said, "Dad?" he jumped.

"Sorry," I told him.

"No, no, it's not you, Casey. I'm on edge, I guess. Come on in. Sit down."

I sat down in one of my favorite armchairs. "I don't want to interrupt your work."

"This isn't *work* work," Dad explained. "I'm still searching for clues about the kingdom of Trewellyn."

"Have you found anything?"

"Nothing." Dad ran his fingers through his hair. "Nada. Zilch. Zippo. I've e-mailed medieval scholars, I posted a picture of the box online to see if any antique experts could identify it . . . and so far I've come up with zero."

"Well, that's weird. But even if Trewellyn doesn't exist, the princess sure does. I can prove that by the mess she makes in our bathroom."

"Speaking of messes," Dad said, "I went by Drew Street again to check out the house where you bought the box. It's been demolished. Not a stick or a stone left, in less than a week. Boy, I wish I'd gotten that contract. . . ."

"Dad?" I said, interrupting him. "You don't *like* the princess, do you?"

"Well . . . I don't hate her," he replied.

"That's not an answer," I said.

He sighed. "Casey, she's vain, arrogant, bossy, occasionally downright rude, and she thinks she's better than everybody else. What's not to like? On the other hand," he continued, "she's rather pretty, and kind of innocent, and sometimes I feel sorry for her.

But that doesn't mean I'm not ready for her to leave."

I felt the same way. "Well, I don't think anyone that rude deserves to be pretty," I complained. It was my turn to sigh. "Dad . . . do you think Mom would be disappointed in me?"

The question startled him and it surprised me a little, too.

"Of course not!" he insisted. "Why would you ever think that?"

"I don't know. I just never feel like I fit in. I don't even know what to say—you know—to boys."

I'm sure I was blushing. *Where did that come from? Why'd I have to go and mention boys to Dad?*

He gave me this sort of stunned deer-in-headlights look, and for a second I was afraid he'd stopped breathing. Then Dad leaned back in his chair and stared at the ceiling. But in the end, he came through for me—he always did.

"Well," Dad said, "at your age, I'm sure your mother could get a little tongue-tied, too. And when *I* was your age, I was only comfortable talking to my dog."

I was speechless. Somehow, I never thought of a guy being the shy one—especially not Dad.

"Give yourself a break, Casey." He looked me right in the eyes. "It takes time to get comfortable with yourself. Years. I know your mom would tell you to be true to yourself, and you are. Every time I watch you play soccer, I feel her sitting there beside me, cheering louder than anybody."

His voice grew softer. "And by the way, you're a beautiful girl. Don't ever sell yourself short, Casey."

Beautiful? I had no idea what to say, so I stared at my worn-out sneakers.

Dad scratched the back of his neck thoughtfully. "I know if your mom were here, she'd be nice to the princess. Nicer than I've been. But she'd be just as confused by the whole thing as we are."

Somehow, talking to Dad had made me even more confused. And not just about the princess. Between Egg at home and Eden and her posse at school, I was surrounded by girlie-girl royalty. And despite what Dad seemed to think, I didn't feel all that great about being myself. Part of me wished I could be just as girlie as Eden, especially when it came to boys. But Dad had been right about one thing—Mom wouldn't want me pretending to be like anyone else. So how could I be me *and* survive life in princess-infested Pine Glen? That was my royal dilemma!

8.

Ye Royal Encounter with Alisha

Thursday came, then Friday, and the weekend was flying by with no sign of Alaric. Not even a toad or a lizard in sight. On Sunday morning, Gran and Dad called me into the kitchen for an emergency meeting.

"Eglantine needs to learn about the world," Gran began. "She's been spending far too much time playing Battle Royal with Shane and watching television."

"I told her to turn off the TV but she banished me from the den," Dad said wearily.

"It's time for her to start school. Now," Gran continued.

"I have an idea." I was desperate. "You can home-school her."

"No, Casey, I don't want to," Gran insisted. "As long as she's here, she should experience normal teenage life."

I wanted to explain that normal teenage life isn't all it's cracked up to be. "Maybe Alaric will find the spell," I said hopefully.

"That's what bothers me the most," Dad admitted. "We haven't set eyes on him all week. Maybe he's not coming back."

My heart sank. Wouldn't you think a wizard would have a pager or something?

"She should go to school with you, Casey," Dad continued. "I already talked to Jack Talbot and he said we could enroll her. He'll write 'documents pending' in her file. He did give me some trouble about a transcript, though."

"What did you tell him?" Gran asked.

"I guess I think like Casey. I said she was home-schooled," Dad said. "She'll start on Monday."

I was ready to sentence myself to the dungeon.

My bad humor carried over to Sunday afternoon, when I met Alisha in the park to blow off some steam by kicking a soccer ball around. After a while we headed over to a bench and sat down to relax.

"Do you think I'm a ball hog?" I blurted out.

"No," she said. "You're twice the player most of the girls on the team are. Of course, I think you could pass to *me* once in a while," she said with a grin.

"So I *am* stingy about passing?"

"I don't blame you for not passing to Lindsey or Heather." Alisha explained. "Lindsey couldn't hit the side of a barn with a ball, and Heather has no power. But you can count on me."

I sighed. "I'm sorry. I'll try harder."

"It's this cousin thing that's bugging you, isn't it?" she asked.

"She's starting school tomorrow," I admitted.

Alisha groaned.

"Wait till you get a load of her," I said. Then I had a brainstorm. "You should stop by later and meet her, so she can get used to being around normal people."

"Am I a normal person?" Alisha asked hopefully.

"Compared with Egg, even I'm normal," I confessed.

She laughed a little too hard but I guess I asked for it.

Before introducing Alisha to the princess, I gave Egg the standard drill: no mention of being a princess, no mention of living in a castle, no sending people to the dungeon. And no dropping names like "my father, the king."

"Prithee, why not?" she asked.

The Pain took pity on me and tried to help. "Think of it as a secret mission. Like James Bond," he told the princess.

"Lord James of Bond?" asked Egg.

"Yeah. Like you're in disguise and nobody's supposed to know who you are," I suggested.

"Oh!" the princess exclaimed. "Like my father, the king! He once disguised himself as a peasant and went into the village so he could mingle with the commoners."

"What did he find out?" Shane asked.

"That everyone loved their king." The princess was getting misty-eyed.

"Here's the important thing to remember. We don't have kings in this country. We have a democracy, where everyone is considered equal," I told her.

From the look on her face, I might as well have said that in our country pigs fly and ducks sing opera.

"Equal to what?" she asked, horrified.

"Each person is equal to another," I told her.

While she was taking that in, Shane explained, "See, the president is kind of like the king except he's a regular guy and he can't stay president forever and he can even get kicked out."

"Or *he* can be a *she*," I reminded him. "All races, religions, and sexes—equal."

"'Tis not possible," the princess whispered. She was so pale, I thought she might faint.

"And there are no princesses at school," I continued. "Except Eden Endicott."

Egg's eyes opened wide. "Who is this Princess Eden? Where is her kingdom?"

"She doesn't have a kingdom but she still thinks she's better than everybody else."

"Does she have a crown?" asked Egg.

"She does fine without one. Anyway, avoid her at all costs," I advised.

Egg frowned. "My father, the king, says where two princesses dwell, there dwells trouble."

"Well, maybe you can banish her from Pine Glen," I said.

That was the best idea I'd had in a long time.

When Alisha walked in, Egg was astonished. "I have never seen anyone with skin so dark," she announced.

"Egg!" I scolded her. My cheeks were hot. *Imagine*—that's the first thing she says to my best friend, whose skin just happens to be a beautiful shade of chocolaty brown.

Alisha was completely unperturbed. "Calm down,

Casey. I was about to say that I've never seen anyone with skin so white. Except maybe in that *Cinderella* movie."

"Who is this Cinderella?" Egg asked.

"You never heard of Cinderella?" Alisha looked stunned.

"She's led a sheltered life. Never even saw TV, till last week," I explained.

Before long, Gran joined the three of us in the den, where we watched *Cinderella* and even sang along. Duke trotted in to join us, plopping himself at Egg's feet, so we'd know he liked her best.

Egg didn't say a single word until the movie was over.

"What did you think?" Alisha asked.

Egg wrinkled her nose. "No self-respecting prince would marry a girl because her foot fit a glass slipper. Besides, he would already have been betrothed to someone of royal lineage."

"Betrothed?" Alisha asked.

"Engaged," I explained. "Eglantine reads a lot of old books."

"In our kingdom," Egg answered, "a prince would be betrothed to a princess at an early age."

Alisha was getting way too interested. "You live in a kingdom?"

I had to stop Egg before she explained about her father, the king, and her own personal wizard. "The place she comes from has very old traditions," I explained lamely.

Egg stared off into space. "I do wish Father would have given me a pair of those glass slippers for my birthday." She turned to Gran. "Do you think the shoe merchant who sold you my pink slippers would sell me a pair?"

"I don't think they make glass slippers anymore, Eglantine. Too many lawsuits, I imagine," Gran replied.

"Are you all set for school, Eggelton?" Alisha asked.

"Eglantine," Egg corrected her. "At first, I thought 'twas a foul idea. But now I am quite looking forward to it. Exchanging ideas with commoners my own age should be quite stimulating."

"Most of the commoners at our school sleep through all that stimulating exchange," I muttered.

"You'll do okay," Alisha assured her. "Just be yourself."

The curse of the princess continued. Now even my best friend was acting a whole lot nicer than she needed to be. Maybe Egg would be okay, but I was pretty sure the week ahead would be less than fine for me.

Especially if the princess decided to *really* be herself.

9.

Ye School Daze

Her Highness, Princess Eglantine of Trewellyn, was almost late to her first day of school, mainly because she couldn't decide whether to wear blue ribbons on her legs and pink streamers in her hair or vice versa.

"Most girls don't wear anything in their hair," I assured her. "Hats aren't allowed at school."

"Well, I must wear something on my head, if not my tiara." She fussed with the streamers. "Oh, I do miss my lady-in-waiting!"

"I'll bet she misses you," I mumbled. "You're such a joy to wait on."

Amazingly, when it was almost time for us to leave, Alaric made a surprise visit, magically appearing in a cloud of purple smoke and knocking over a Chinese vase in the front hall. Luckily Gran caught it in midair.

"Good catch," I told her. "We could use you in the outfield next spring."

"My word, that was almost like magic," the wizard said admiringly.

Alaric's timing *was* magic. Here was my dream come true: Alaric appearing in the nick of time to whisk the princess back to Trewellyn and out of our lives forever. And no one at Pine Glen Junior High would ever know she existed, except Alisha!

"Alaric—have you got the spell?" I asked breathlessly.

The wizard stroked his chin. "Spell? Aye, I have the spell."

I think my heart did a cartwheel.

"But it still doesn't work."

I groaned.

"Don't worry. You'll get it one of these days, Alaric," Gran said.

"I remain optimistic. If at first you don't succeed and all that." He attempted a chuckle, but it fell pretty flat.

Gran excused herself to get the princess moving. "Don't want her to be late for her first day of school," she explained.

"Well, this *is* a big day." Alaric beamed like a proud big brother.

"Yeah, I hardly slept a wink, I was so excited." It was partially true. "Alaric, if you can't warp Egg back to Trewellyn, can you at least cast a spell to make her act and talk like a twenty-first-century girl?"

Alaric looked puzzled.

"No hair ribbons?" I asked. "No castles, kings, or dungeons?"

"Ah, I see. That is entirely possible. I could cast the Time and Space Harmonizing Spell."

I was about to sigh a great sigh of relief when Alaric wagged a finger in the air. "Except that spell simply does not work on princesses. Princes either."

It figured.

Egg and Gran showed up at last. After Alaric admired Egg's goofy getup, we headed out the door. My heart felt as if it had sunk to my shoes and it wasn't easy to walk.

As Gran unlocked the car, Alaric leaned in close and whispered in my ear. "I thank you. You have just given me an idea of great importance."

Whoopee. I just hoped the smell of cinnamon and ginger wouldn't hang around me all day. Alaric's gingerbread scent was making me hungry.

Though she held her head high, I detected a little chink in the princess's armor when she first saw the school building.

"'Tis enormous, Casey! How many students inhabit it?"

"How many students *are* there," I corrected her. "About eight hundred."

She looked around, wide-eyed. "Larger than all of Trewellyn—but no moat, no drawbridge. Oh, well, the more, the merrier—'tis a saying my father, the king, invented."

"I know the saying, and please don't mention your father—remember?"

The princess sighed.

We stopped by the office to get Egg's transfer cards and her locker assignment. As I expected, from the first moment she walked down the hall, Egg got plenty of attention. Stares, snickers, catcalls— you name it. Two seventh graders actually collided in the hall because they were gaping at Egg instead of watching where they were going.

"Doesn't it bug you—the way everyone is looking at you?" I asked as I showed her to her locker.

The princess leaped backward and flicked an imaginary insect off her arm. "Bug? Begone, despicable pest!"

"Relax. 'Bug' means 'bother.' Doesn't all this

attention bother you?"

Egg smiled mysteriously. "One cannot be a princess without attracting attention. Besides, *they* are merely peasants. They do not understand royal protocol."

"Neither do I," I admitted glumly.

"I know." Egg flashed her superior smile.

"Check out the new girl," I heard Albert Falutti say.

"Must be Halloween," Noah Chung quipped as they passed by. "Not bad, though."

Mr. Talbot had been thoughtful enough to arrange for the princess to have the same exact schedule as mine. I grumpily made a mental note to thank him as I steeled myself for what could only be a disaster of a day.

English class was first. It was hard enough to face Mrs. Markle at 7:30 on an ordinary morning, but with Egg around, I didn't know what to expect.

Mrs. Markle was as straight up and down as an exclamation point. When a student didn't know an answer, her eyebrows wiggled like apostrophes. Mrs. Markle loved punctuation, grammar, and books, of course.

"People, we have a new pupil today." Mrs. Markle referred to the card in her hand. "Eglantine Peabody. My, what a lovely, old-fashioned name. Do you have a nickname?"

Egg frowned. "Nickname? I do not understand."

"I thought maybe you went by something shorter," Mrs. Markle said. "Like Tina."

I held my breath.

"Eglantine is my short name. My full name is Eglantine Eleanor Annalisa Ambrosia de Bercy . . ."

"Peabody," I added quickly before she could get to the Trewellyn part.

Naturally there were giggles.

"Well, that is an impressive name. So, I hope you will all welcome Eggoton . . ."

Mrs. Markle's eyebrows bounced up and down a few times as she consulted the transfer card and corrected herself. "Welcome *Eglantine* . . . to our class. Today we're discussing literature related to King Arthur and the Round Table," Mrs. Markle explained.

"King Arthur?" the princess repeated. "What kingdom does he rule?"

"Camelot," Mrs. Markle answered. "Today we're going to discuss a poem called 'The Lady of Shalott' by Alfred, Lord Tennyson. If you want to skim over the poem as we do, perhaps you can catch up, Eglantine."

"Lord Tennyson? Does he live here in Pine Glen?"

I winced as snickers erupted around the room. Egg didn't bat an eyelash.

"No, he lived in England back in the nineteenth century." Before the princess could ask any more questions, Mrs. Markle asked, "Now, class, who would like to sum up the poem for us in a few sentences?" Only Jon Dooley's hand waved, but naturally, the teacher ignored the only kid in the room who knew the answer. Instead, she called on Noah.

"I didn't get it," he answered with a shrug. "I thought this class was supposed to be English, but I didn't understand a word of this thing."

"Well, some of the language is a little archaic, but it is written in English and I did provide you with a glossary. Anyone else?"

Jon's hand waved like a flag but Mrs. Markle didn't seem to see it. "Casey Peabody—how about you?"

Busted! It was the first time in the school year she'd called on me and it never would have happened if Egg hadn't drawn her attention to me. I glanced over at my so-called cousin, but she was concentrating on reading the poem.

I took a deep breath. "Well, there's this Lady of Shalott who lives in a tower on an island and there's a curse on her so she's not supposed to look directly down at Camelot."

I hesitated so she could correct me, but Mrs. Markle just motioned for me to continue.

"So she watches everything in a mirror as people

come and go to Camelot. But one day Sir Lancelot comes along and—I don't know why—but he gets her attention and she looks directly down on Camelot."

"That's fairly accurate, Casey. Go on."

I took another deep breath. "So she knows that's the end, I guess. They never really say how she knows she's doomed, but she gets a boat and writes her name on it."

The teacher interrupted. "Which is?"

"The Lady of Shalott. And she just gets in the boat and lies down and floats to Camelot and dies."

"Very good. And then Sir Lancelot . . . ?"

"Well, he sees her and says, like, that she's really pretty and he kind of blesses her?"

I hadn't said so much in class in my whole life.

Mrs. Markle began to expand on what I said when suddenly Egg let out a loud moan.

"Eglantine? Is something wrong?"

Egg was so pale, I was afraid she was going to pass out. "'Tis the saddest thing I ever read!" Then she composed herself. "I am deeply sorry for my outburst. I promise to control myself henceforth."

Snickers, giggles, whispers.

"No, don't! I'm glad to find someone so moved by poetry. Tell me, what makes you so sad?"

"Oh, 'tis so lonely to be in a tower, to be sentenced to a life with no hope of human intercourse. . . ."

Howls, hoots, chaos. I must have turned beet red.

Mrs. Markle clapped her hands. "Class, please! If you don't know that the word 'intercourse' means communication among people, you should!"

More whispers. My face was plum purple. Even Mrs. Markle had turned a little pink. Egg just looked pale and bewildered.

"Eglantine, I'm very impressed with how quickly you were able to get to the heart of the poem. Didn't the language give you difficulty?"

"To the contrary. It is much more sensible than the local dialect," she said.

Oh, to be invisible! Mercifully the bell rang, and I steered Egg out of the room as fast as possible.

"Well, *that* was embarrassing," I muttered as we hurried to the next class. "And humiliating and . . . mortifying."

"Yes," Egg agreed. "A princess is not supposed to show emotion. I must curb my tendency to romanticize."

"Yeah, you really should."

Mr. Jablonski welcomed Egg to chorus class, though he also had a hard time pronouncing her name. He asked her if she would sing a piece of her choice to help him figure out where to place her. He was taken aback when she chose a catchy tune called "Stay Ye Out of the Dell This Morrow."

"Uh . . . nice voice," he said. "Do you play any instruments?"

"The lute," Egg answered.

"The flute?"

"No! The lute. You strum it thusly." Egg pretended to play some kind of guitar-like instrument.

"Oh, the lute!" said Mr. Jablonski.

"A tiresome instrument," Egg continued. I tensed up, wondering where this was going. "Almost as bad as embroidering tapestries all day."

There were a few snickers in the room but most of the kids in the class didn't understand a thing she said. Lutes and tapestries might as well have been communicable diseases.

Mr. Jablonski quickly placed Egg in the soprano section. (Thankfully, I'm an alto.)

Algebra followed chorus. I could have hugged Ms. Espinoza because she merely found a seat for Egg and spent the rest of class time writing equations on the board. I was never so happy to hear a teacher drone on before. I dared look at the princess only once. She sat straight in her chair with her hands folded on the desk. From the expression on her face,

I could tell she didn't understand a word.

"What language was she speaking?" she asked afterward.

"I guess you haven't had algebra yet," I said as we hurried toward history class.

"There is no need for such nonsense when you have a royal mathematician," she replied without embarrassment.

I was too busy thinking about how useful a royal mathematician would be to notice the stares and giggles directed our way in the hallway.

Okay, I did hear someone say, "Is she serious?" Somebody else said, "Call the fashion police." But the princess remained unruffled.

I had a nagging feeling about history, with good reason as it turned out. Mr. Hibble had a thing about maps. Since Egg had already informed me that the earth was flat, I was sure there was trouble ahead.

"Ah, we have another Ms. Peabody," he said when Egg handed him her transfer card. "Are you two related?"

"Distantly," I quickly responded. After all, seven hundred years is quite a distance.

Once class was started, Mr. Hibble asked Egg to show the class where she came from. The princess stared at the large map, baffled.

Feet shuffled, throats were cleared, papers rustled while Egg studied the map.

Mr. Hibble finally spoke. "Ms. Peabody?"

"'Tis not here," she explained.

"Well, where are you from?" the teacher asked.

"Trewellyn," she said.

The tension was getting to me. "I don't think it's on the map. It's tiny."

Egg pivoted around and gave me a withering glare. "'Tis a *huge* kingdom."

"Kingdom?" Mr. Hibble asked skeptically.

I had to fake it. "Kingdom High School, Trewellyn, California. Near, uh, Sacramento."

Mr. Hibble took off his glasses and leaned in close to the top of California. "No Trewellyn here. I'll have to do some research. Now . . . shall we get back to ancient Babylon?"

The crisis was averted and to my relief, Egg stayed quiet for the rest of class. But the day was only half over, and I was afraid we weren't out of the woods yet. Alas, for once, I was right!

10.

Ye Chilly First Impressions

I dreaded lunch most of all. I longed to abandon the princess, but Gran had made me promise to stick with her every minute of the day.

When we entered the lunchroom, Egg stopped dead in her tracks. I guess she'd never seen so many peasants in one place before.

"Just do what I do," I told her. "Remember, you're in disguise."

"Like Lord James of Bond," she replied mysteriously.

I looked around for Alisha and almost dropped my tray when I saw her sitting with a group of kids, laughing hysterically, gathered around the class clown, Aceman Paceman. I almost gagged. I guess hanging out at the Pizza Palace had paid off for her.

After I steered Egg through the line, I found us a quiet corner so I could teach her the fine art of holding a taco without the insides falling out. It was such an intricate process, I didn't even notice Maddy Ames and Tino Abruzzo stopping by our table.

"Hi, Casey. This is, like, your cousin?" Maddy asked in her squeaky voice. I swear she sounded like a chipmunk. She and I weren't what you'd call friends, but we'd been in the same classes all through elementary and middle school.

"Kind of. Maddy, Tino, meet Eglantine."

"Eglantine—yo! Maybe you should change your name to Eglan*tino*," Tino joked. He was a sweet guy, a football player. A halfback, no less.

"I was wondering . . . do people really dress like that where you're from?" Maddy asked. "I've never seen clothes like yours."

"I should be thrown into the dungeon for dressing like this," Egg replied. "Where I come from, not even the peasants would wear the clothes of this kingdom!"

I held my breath. Egg's whole cover was about to be blown, as well as any remote chance I had of being considered normal.

Suddenly Tino laughed. "That's cool how she talks! Peasants—that's cool."

"Yeah," said Maddy. "A real comic. But that name—Eggletine—it's hard to say."

"Well, you could call me the prin . . ."

I stopped her just in time. "Egg. It's shorter."

"Egg!" Tino chortled again. "I like it! Egg and peasants, that sounds cool."

"It sounds warm to me," Egg responded.

Tino snorted with laughter. "You're killing me!"

"I am? Well, off with your head!"

No matter what came out of Egg's mouth, Tino thought she was a comic genius! Since Maddy had a huge crush on Tino, she pretended to think Egg was a genius, too. Finally Egg laughed along with them, even though I knew she had no idea what was so funny.

"Why were they laughing?' she asked as the bell rang and we headed to our next class.

"Because they thought you were joking. You know, being funny."

She gasped in horror. "Princesses are not funny."

Boy, she had that right.

Although I usually complain that our lunch break seems way too short, that day I was almost relieved to get to French class (even though I always had trouble getting my tongue around those *r*'s).

Egg seemed unusually relaxed after her lunch, which made me nervous. "You know where France is?"

She gave me that cold royal smile and said, "*Oui, naturellement.*"

At this point, Monsieur Dobkins entered. Even though he looked about as French as a leprechaun, he insisted on being called "Monsieur." Everyone called him "M."—the abbreviation for Monsieur—behind his back.

"*Bonjour!*" M. said cheerily. He picked up the transfer card on his desk and examined it.

"*Ah, une nouvelle élève!*" His eyes scanned the classroom until he saw Egg sitting regally in the back row. She might as well have been sitting on a throne.

"*Vous vous appelez . . .*" He squinted at the card. "*Mademoiselle Eglantine?*"

"*Oui, monsieur. Je m'appelle Eglantine.*"

"*Bonjour, mademoiselle,*" he replied. "*Comment allez-vous?*"

"*Bien, merci, et vous?*" she responded. About that time, a bunch of kids turned in their seats to check out the princess.

"*Bien. Quel jour sommes-nous?*" the teacher asked. I thought he'd asked something about what day it was.

"*Lundi, monsieur,*" Egg answered. Monday.

"*Bon! Où habitez-vous?*" M. asked.

"Where do I live?" Egg translated.

I sucked in my breath. M. had led us into dangerous territory. I steeled myself for the word "Trewellyn," or worse, "*le roi,*" which I knew meant the king.

Instead I heard, "*J'habite chez ma cousine Casey Peabody.*"

Whew. No *Trewellyn*. No *roi*. I'm no expert, but I could tell that Egg's French sounded a lot more French than the teacher's. I think he realized it as well and quickly switched to English. "You speak French very well!"

Egg flashed him a mysterious smile. "Does not everyone, monsieur?"

M. laughed nervously. "No, mademoiselle. But they should!"

Was I jealous of Egg? *Naturellement*. But I was also impressed. *Quel* weird, *non?*

In sixth-period science class, Ms. Speckles didn't make a big fuss about the new student. She was too busy preparing us for our first lab. Egg seemed unusually fascinated by the rows of beakers and Bunsen burners.

"You did not tell me that the teacher is a wizard," she whispered excitedly on our way out of the class-room.

"Believe me, she's not," I assured her. "There are no wizards anymore."

"Oh," she said in a snotty tone of voice. "That's right. 'Tis a pity so much scientific knowledge has been lost. 'Tis an age of darkness I have found myself in."

My fists were clenched. So were my teeth. After a whole day with the princess, I was ready to ditch her and flee to soccer practice. But Egg was still unclear on the concept of books and lockers and I had to help her with her combination lock.

"I don't see why I must carry this knapsack like a peasant," she complained.

"For all your books," I told her.

"I don't see why I must carry so many books home with me."

I started piling the books in her backpack like a lady-in-waiting. "Because you have homework."

Before she could protest, I grabbed her backpack and started walking. "Come on. Gran will be waiting out front." I was hurrying her toward the front door when I heard an earsplitting chorus of high-pitched giggles. Stupid me, I turned to see who was laughing. It was Eden Endicott and the usual suspects: Sabrina

Toth and Kiki Green, all staring at Egg and snickering. I knew there was no point in saying anything to them, but the princess didn't know better. She looked Eden dead in the eye.

"Greetings," she said with a frosty smile. "Something must be most wonderfully amusing."

They burst into full chuckles (not ladylike ones, either). Eden composed herself enough to say, "We were admiring those ribbons or whatever they are on your legs."

More giggles.

"I am pleased that you like them. I think they are rather chilly, myself."

I nudged her hard with my elbow and whispered, "Cool."

It was too late. "Chilly!" screeched Sabrina. "She said *chilly*!"

The princess took a few steps toward them, still holding her head high. "I am Eglantine Peabody. And this is my cousin Casey."

"Oh, I know your cousin." Eden's voice dripped with sarcasm.

"And who might you be?" Egg continued.

Eden and her friends were forced to introduce themselves and the princess perked up when she heard Eden's name. "Ah, 'tis the *other* princess," she said. Then she held her chin high and swept out the door, toward Gran's waiting car.

I was left facing the most popular girl in school. "What was *that*?" Eden asked with a smirk.

"My cousin," I replied. I stuck my chin up in the air as if I were wearing a tiara, and hurried off to soccer practice.

After dragging Egg around all day, followed by a full soccer practice, I was exhausted and starving when I got home. Thank goodness Gran had cooked up her famous spaghetti and meatballs, a favorite of all us Peabodys.

"What is this?" the princess demanded to know. "It looks like the nest of a dragon!"

"Oh! So you have dragons in Trewellyn?" Dad asked with a twinkle in his eye.

"We *did*. The Great One caused terrible problems for our kingdom until my father, the king, slew him." The girl was dead serious.

"Tell me, Princess, did you ever actually see this dragon?" Dad asked slyly.

"No, but it caused raging fires across the countryside," Egg replied.

"Thunderstorms hitting dry grass." Dad winked at Shane and me. "So, Princess, when your father, the king, killed the dragon, did you see the body?"

"No," said Egg. "It was too huge to drag such a long distance. He did bring back a flask of dragon's blood."

"What'd it look like?" Shane asked.

"Dark red." Egg's tone was defiant. She sensed she was being tested. "And after my father slew the dragon, the fires ceased."

"Chicken blood," Dad suggested. "Then the rains came."

Gran frowned. "Now, Joseph."

"He did bring home a dragon claw," Egg announced.

Dad was clearly dubious. "How big was it?"

Egg held her hands up a good three feet apart. "This big. And sharp as a knight's best sword."

"You saw it?" Shane's eyes looked as big as saucers.

Egg nodded. "Of course. Ask Alaric. Ask the duke."

I heard Duke's tail thumping from his favorite spot under the table.

Shane let out a huge sigh. "I sure wish you'd brought that claw with you."

"The spateggi, 'tis delicious," the princess said. "'Tis chilly!"

Gran frowned and I quickly explained. "She means cool. As in good—right?"

The princess nodded as she took another generous fork full.

"*All* Gran's cooking is chilly," Dad said.

"Precisely," the princess agreed. "I shall take your formula to the royal cook when I return."

Sure thing, I thought to myself. *Leave now and I'll pack you a doggy bag.*

11.

Ye New Guy

I have to admit I was surprised and relieved that Egg got through a whole day of school without sending someone to the dungeon or mentioning her father, the king. Still, I knew there was dangerous territory ahead, because on Tuesday we had P.E.

"I shan't be seen in those," she protested when I gave her the T-shirt, shorts, and running shoes. "Why, even a wee babe would not be seen in such skimpy garments in Trewellyn. And these boots are most ugly!"

"Luckily we aren't in Trewellyn. And if you don't wear these clothes, Coach Curson will go on a rampage."

"Who is he?" Egg asked, holding the T-shirt away from her body as if it were a disease.

"*She,*" I replied. "Remember: She has a whistle and she's not afraid to use it."

Egg sighed. "Can you not vote her out?" she asked.

I guess I'd defined democracy a tad too narrowly. "The *country* is a democracy. *School* is not."

Gran bustled into the room. "There you are, Princess. My, you'll look like a real Pine Glen Panther."

"Maybe you'd better practice getting in and out of those sneaks, Princess. Just to save you some embarrassment in P.E. tomorrow." I meant *my* embarrassment, of course.

Let me tell you, I remember having trouble learning to tie my shoes when I was four but you can't imagine how much trouble Egg had learning to tie *hers.* Gran was patient; I was not.

"Casey, you're not helping," Gran finally said. "Why don't you go do your homework?"

Homework was almost a relief after watching a teenage girl struggle to tie her own shoes. But homework was not a concept that came easily to the princess, either. Later, when I pointed out that she had some math problems due the next day, she said, "Perfectly ridiculous. Whoever thought up this homework nonsense should be banished from the kingdom!"

For once, she had a point. I dug into my math but the pile of books on the princess's bed were of no interest to her. She had something else on her mind.

"Casey, may I ask you about your attire?"

I could pretty much guess what was coming. Let me explain. When I'm playing soccer or softball, I wear a uniform, and I wear a different kind of uniform the rest of the time. I wear jeans, shorts, or sweatpants, depending on the weather, a soccer or baseball jersey, and a baseball cap. I wear my hair in a ponytail with an elastic band around it or, when I'm playing soccer, a long braid. My footwear of choice: sneakers or sandals. I've been known to wear a skirt, but only when Gran insists. It's my choice.

Still, I cringed when Egg said, "I do not understand why you dress most mannishly. You are comely enough, for a commoner."

Maybe I was supposed to take that as a compliment.

"I'm not the tiara type," I told her. "I'm comfortable with what I wear."

"One might be comfortable in a corset and knickers but I wouldn't think it proper to attend school like that. Though some maidens I saw today wore little more."

"Do you think I should dress like you?" I managed to leave out the words "silly," "stupid," and "ridiculous."

"Oh no. My attire would not befit you. I think you should dress like *you*."

I tugged on the top of my jersey. "This is me. I'm a soccer player."

The princess lifted her nose in the air. "Pish posh. If soccer were outlawed tomorrow, you would still be Casey Peabody. Then what would you dress like?"

"A softball player," I shot back.

I stuck my nose back in my math book. The conversation was over. Egg rose with a sigh and announced, "I intend to search through your grandmother's treasure chests on your behalf."

On my own behalf, I intended not to care.

When Egg and I got to school the next morning, all eyes were on us as we walked down the hallway. We might as well have been walking the red carpet at one of those Hollywood award shows. The attention was understandable—the princess had totally outdone herself. This time, she wore a short gold skirt—originally a tablecloth—with a triangle of lace tied around it at an angle. She wore a lace blouse, a piece of green velvet ribbon around her neck, and yesterday's gold belt was today's headband. The ribbons tied around her legs were emerald green.

My face was bright red.

"Check out the legs." That was either a chipmunk speaking or it was Maddy.

"Yeah—she has awesome legs." That was Tino.

"I'm talking about the dorky ribbons."

Tino was all innocence. "What ribbons?"

I gave Egg a sharp jab in the ribs. "Everybody's staring at you," I whispered, hoping Egg would realize how outlandish she looked.

"Of course they're staring. They always do. *I* am the princess." She raised her head even higher and smiled at what she thought were her admiring subjects.

And I'm *your lady-in-waiting,* I thought. *Waiting for you to disappear.*

I held my breath through all our morning classes and with good reason. In English, we got through the discussion of Alfred, Lord Tennyson, okay. But when Mrs. Markle brought up King Arthur and the Knights of the Round Table again, the princess's hand shot up immediately.

"I thought you had no kings in this country," Egg said with a hint of suspicion in her voice.

I closed my eyes as the snickers started.

"This poem is set in England."

"I certainly never heard of a Round Table," the princess protested. "Ours is square."

Mrs. Markle raised a sharp eyebrow. "King Arthur wanted to sit among his knights as their equal."

Egg responded with a loud "Ha!"

All heads turned to stare at her.

"He is the king and they are merely knights. They are not equals. Now, my father . . ."

I had to act fast. "Mrs. Markle, I think Eglantine is confused." The teacher and princess both glared at me. "She thinks King Arthur was a real person, not a guy in a book."

"Some experts do think he was real," Mrs. Markle answered. "There are many interesting books on the subject. Perhaps you'd like to do some extra-credit reading."

"Perhaps I shall," said Egg. Her blue eyes had turned a stormy gray. "Though I do not think I shall like it."

After English came P.E., the period I'd really been dreading. Egg managed to change into her gym clothes (without a servant to help her). Sneaker-tying, however, took a lot out of her. She finally succeeded with a combination of concentration and perspiration. I'd never seen her sweat before.

"Hurry, Egg," I urged her as Coach Curson's whistle pierced the air.

"Did you call her *Egg*?" Lindsey Malick asked. She's one of the klutzier members of the soccer team.

"I meant Eglantine," I explained.

"Egg is cooler. I like it!" she said.

The princess was completely mystified. "She thinks the name Egg is chilly?" she whispered to me.

I didn't bother to remind her the word was "cool."

We hit the field and Coach hit the whistle again.

"New girl?" she bellowed.

Egg stopped in her tracks. "Me? I'm the pr—"

I jabbed her in the ribs. Harder, this time.

"New girl, Eggula! What's with the gift wrapping on your bean?" Coach never minced words.

The princess was totally bewildered.

"She means the ribbons in your hair," I whispered.

"Well, 'tis my adornment," Egg answered.

Coach glared at her. "Lose it for gym class."

"I cannot! I would feel naked without some adornment. In my castle . . ."

"She went to Castle High," I interrupted. "Trewellyn, California."

Coach Curson tried to stare down the princess but Egg held her own.

"Try to keep them out of everyone's eyes," Coach said. Then she blew her whistle right in Egg's face to get the class moving.

Coach always liked to start things off by getting everyone to break into a sweat. "Twice around the track," she yelled. Under normal circumstances I would have charged ahead of the pack. But I stuck by Egg's side, trying to get her to run at least a little faster than a tortoise.

"Haven't you ever run before?"

"No!" As Egg took dainty, mincing steps across the cinders, Coach Curson gave another mighty blast on her whistle.

"Pick up the pace back there," she barked.

"You've got to run faster," I told her.

"Princesses don't run," Egg pronounced firmly.

"What if a dragon were chasing you?"

Egg's eyes grew wide. "I have never been chased by a dragon."

"Well, there's one behind us now. Let's go—or we're toast!" I dashed ahead but when I peeked back, Egg was really running at last, her ribbons all aflutter.

"That's more like it, new girl!" Coach cried out. "Now you've got some fire in that fanny!"

Egg actually looked worried. "Casey? What is her meaning?"

"Believe it or not, that was a compliment," I assured her as, together, we overtook the two girls in front of us. Then, to my utter amazement, Egg sprinted ahead of me.

"New girl! Eggletine!" Coach Curson called out. "You run track before?"

Egg was clearly puzzled. "I do not believe so."

"Well, you're running track now," Coach announced. "Come spring, you're officially on the team."

Later, back at my locker, I was still trying to figure out how the princess managed to outrun me when suddenly, this guy I'd never seen before came right up to me. The really shocking thing: He was totally *cute*.

There was something familiar about him. Those green eyes, maybe? And he was grinning like he knew me.

"Hey, Case, how's it going?" he asked, still grinning. I tried not to freak out and reached for my French book.

"Looks like Egg really made a splash," he added.

My mind was reeling. "Do I know you?" I asked.

He laughed. "Does the name Alaric ring a bell?"

Just then, a lizard peeked out from the pocket of

his backpack, I caught a whiff of cinnamon and ginger, and somebody—or something—said, "Ribbit."

"Alaric?" I whispered.

"In the flesh. Boricius is still working on the spell, so I thought I'd come watch over the princess." He pointed to his clothes. "What do you think of my new look? Sure beats those hot robes."

I was slowly beginning to put the pieces together. The wizard had turned himself into a lanky teenager with wavy brown hair, a wide smile, and eyes as green as the outfield at Dodger Stadium.

"Not bad," I said, trying not to stare. "But that name won't work around here. How about Al? Or Ric?"

He thought it over. "Ric. I like it!"

"How did you do it? You look—you talk—you know—normal."

"It was your idea. You asked about a spell that could make the princess act and talk like somebody from the twenty-first century. It doesn't work on princesses, but for wizards, it's as easy as fee-fi-fo-fum!" His eyes quickly lost their sparkle. "If only getting the princess back home could be so simple."

I glanced at my watch. "Eek—now I'm going to be late! Can you stop time, too?"

"That's Basic Wizardry 101. How long do you want? Five minutes?"

"Two would do."

"Done. The bell won't ring. Yet."

I slammed my locker door and hurried toward French class with Ric at my side.

"Are you going to class?" I asked him.

"I'm . . . like you say . . . hanging out."

"They'll kick you out if they find out you're not enrolled," I warned.

Ric chuckled. "Ah! That's where the Veil of Invisibility comes in. The only people who can see me are the people I *want* to see me. I let the other kids see me—they're pretty friendly, Casey. But the principal and the rest of the staff have no idea I'm here. Even if I mess up and they spot me, I'll perform a Mind Muddle—that's a simple spell that confuses the mind. A person may ask me a question but before I answer, he'll forget he ever asked."

"Could work," I replied. "The principal is pretty muddled already."

Like Ric promised, I made it to the door of my French class in time.

"Thanks for the help. Where will you be?" I asked.

Ric glanced through the door. "Probably up . . . there." He pointed to the top of a large bookcase. "*Au revoir!*"

Poof. He was gone. I rushed inside and slid into

my seat, just as the bell rang.

"Who were you talking to out there?" Egg whispered.

"A guy."

I don't know why Egg looked surprised.

We had a pop quiz in French. Egg got every answer right. I got a 78 percent. You can hardly blame me. I couldn't stop staring at the top of the bookcase. At first, I couldn't see him, but there was a loud "ribbit" during the test. Aceman Paceman got in trouble for it, even though he swore he hadn't done it. For once, he was completely serious.

The next time I looked up, there was Ric, legs folded, sitting near the ceiling and smiling directly at me.

I felt positively chilly.

12.
Ye Boyfriend

By the time I got home from soccer practice, Ric was settled in Shane's room, all wrapped up in Battle Royal. The princess was in our room, sewing an outfit guaranteed to embarrass me. I headed out to Gran's house in the backyard.

"How's it going, honey?" she asked.

I flopped down on her daybed. "Egg's the laughingstock of the school and guess what that makes me? She wears ridiculous clothes, she says ridiculous things, and she acts soooo superior. She's never going to make friends."

"She must be friends with somebody because she got a call."

Not possible. "Who was it?"

"A boy named Tino. He was asking about a homework assignment but they were on the phone for almost an hour."

"Tino! Maddy will kill her!"

"The princess seemed quite pleased."

Tino was a cute jock who probably never thought twice about a homework assignment. Could it be that he had the hots for the Ice Princess?

"If she talked an hour, she must have blown her cover." I was sure Egg couldn't talk that long without mentioning her father, the king.

"It didn't sound like they were talking about Trewellyn," Gran answered with a mysterious smile. "Now, tell me what you think of our Ric. He showed up here after school. Can you believe he's really Alaric?"

"He's sure a lot cuter." I don't know why my cheeks felt hot when I said that. "But I wish he'd concentrate on getting Egg out of here instead of playing computer games."

"I don't think the princess was too thrilled to have him at school, but I convinced her he was only there to help her. He told me that he'll be splitting his time between Pine Glen and Trewellyn."

"Isn't our house getting a little crowded?" I asked.

"Your father's a builder, sweetie. He can always add on."

Great. Maybe he could install a drawbridge while he's at it. And a barbican. I'd looked that one up. It turns out to be extra defense to keep people out. People like princesses!

By the end of Egg's first week at Pine Glen Junior High, a funny—no, *amazing*—thing happened. Instead of snickering at the princess and her weird clothes, people started smiling and saying, "Hi." As in "Hi, Egg! Great shoes." Or "Hi, Egg. Coming to the Spirit Club meeting?"

Nobody invited me.

Tino hung around the princess's locker between classes and after school. He was more than happy to help her with her locker combination. *Oh yeah*—he was hooked.

Egg wasn't the only new popular kid. Everybody at Pine Glen seemed to know Ric, too, and he knew everybody by name. He was high-fiving everyone from Aceman to Ralph Heinie (who, despite his unfortunate name, was a nice guy). But even though he had a flood of new friends, Ric was usually at the door when I came out of class, ready to walk me to the next one. "Hi, Ric. Hi, Casey," we'd be greeted in the hall. No one except me seemed to notice the occasional "ribbit" coming from his backpack.

On Friday, when I got home from soccer practice, my royal roomie said, "Casey, I know not why you say people at school are unfriendly. They have been most kind to me." Ric obviously agreed with her. She carefully removed her tiara from my shelf and placed it on her head. She still liked to wear it around the house.

"Yeah. People seem to like you," I grudgingly admitted.

"Of course they like me. *I* am the princess!"

That kind of talk made me nervous. "They don't know you're a princess, do they?"

"No, but they can tell I am special," she replied without a hint of embarrassment.

"What about Tino?" I asked warily. "Did you tell him?"

"Of course not! Commoners cannot be friends with royalty. He would surely be crushed. But he does not have to know." She tilted her chin up as she admired her profile in the mirror. "Do you think some paint on my lips would look good?"

"You mean lipstick? That stuff is gross!" I replied.

"Why do you say that, Casey?"

"Because it's gross to put a layer of glop on your face. I like the natural look."

"The boys seem to like painted girls," she observed. "I will wager even Ric does."

"Ric?"

"He seems to hang around you a lot," said the princess, running a finger around her rosy lips. "In fact, he spends way too much time with you. He is, after all, *my* wizard."

"He's just being polite. You have nothing to worry about," I muttered.

"I am not worrying, Casey. When it comes to boys, I think I am like you. I can take them or leave them."

Gran poked her head in the door, waving the portable phone. "Phone call for you, Princess. It's Tino. Again."

Egg grabbed the phone and raced out the door, positively cooing.

"He must really like her," said Gran. "Is he a nice boy?"

"Yes," I conceded. "Not the sharpest knife in the drawer. A good athlete, even a good runner for a guy his size. Come to think of it, Egg's a pretty good runner, too. Isn't that weird?"

"She's just a normal teenage girl," said Gran.

"Normal?" I screeched. "She's a medieval

princess! There's nothing *normal* about that."

"You're right, of course. There are moments when things seem so normal, I forget how unusual it is." Gran sighed. "Your father and I need to have a heart-to-heart talk with Alaric."

I relaxed for the first time all week. "Tell him to light a fire under Boricius."

At bedtime, I pretended to be sleepy, gave a big fake yawn, and turned out my light. The princess followed suit, but as I was staring up at the light reflecting off my clock radio, she broke the silence.

"Casey, have you noticed his eyes?"

"Sure," I replied, picturing the intense green orbs that sometimes flashed and sometimes simmered in my daydreams.

"Big and brown, like those giant chocolate chips in Gran's cookies," Egg said dreamily.

Chocolate? Oh. Not Ric. Tino.

"The duke has eyes like that," Egg continued.

"Tino *is* kind of a puppy dog," I admitted. "Sweet. Loyal." I bit my tongue to keep from saying "dumb." Besides, it's not like Tino's really dumb. He's just . . . uncomplicated.

The princess sighed deeply. "Prince Vorland's eyes are pale and watery. He resembles a fish, with his big mouth gulping air. He wheezes, you know."

I turned on my side. "Who's Prince Vorland?"

"My betrothed."

"Your *who*?"

"My future husband," Egg explained. "He has a spotty face. Casey, what am I to do? When I return to Trewellyn, I am due to wed this—geek. Help me, I implore you!"

I was stunned. First of all, I wasn't sure if "geek" was a medieval word or if she'd just picked it up at school. Second of all, nobody ever asked me for advice about boys before. Not even Alisha. I flicked on the light. "Can't you say no?"

The princess looked pale in the harsh light of the table lamp.

"Perhaps you can marry anyone you like, but I am expected to make a marriage favorable for my country. 'Tis my duty."

"Did your parents get married for the good of the country?"

"Oh no. I mean yes," she answered. "Their parents arranged the union but something unheard of happened."

"What?"

"They fell in love!"

I sat on the edge of my bed. "Then your father should understand about Prince Vorland. You deserve to fall in love if you want to. You should even be allowed to skip marriage altogether. It's totally your call."

The princess gasped with shock. "An unmarried princess would be a disgrace! Besides, I owe it to Father. Mother died before she had a chance to produce a male heir, so 'tis up to me."

I assured her that not being married didn't exactly hold back Queen Elizabeth I of England.

"I must learn more about this queen," Egg said. "Still, if it were not for Father, I might not go back at all."

Even though I felt sorry for Egg's plight, I wasn't ready to encourage her to stay. "Maybe Prince Vorland has found somebody else since you've been gone."

She shook her head. "You have not seen Prince Vorland."

There was a knock at the door. "Everything okay in there?" It was Dad checking in on us.

"We're just talking, Dad. Girl talk."

"Thank you, Your Dadness," Egg said sweetly.

He said good-bye and we heard him shuffle away.

Egg settled back on her pillows and placed her tiara on her head. "What of your parents? Why did they marry?"

"It was love, that's for sure." I took a photo in a

silver frame out of the drawer of my nightstand. "Here's their wedding picture." I handed it to the princess.

She eagerly studied the photo. "Your mother is beautiful—like a queen. And his dadness was so handsome!" She studied it a long time before handing it back. "'Twas love, all right, Casey. I can see it in their eyes. Gran told me how sick your mother was and how you all grieved."

Gran told her all that? I was sad, I was mad, and my cheeks were getting very hot. I don't cry in front of other people, except for Gran, and I was determined not to let Egg see me get all weepy.

"At least you have a photo of her." The princess patted her tiara. "I have my mother's jewels, but little else."

"Do you remember her?" I asked.

"I remember that she was beautiful," Egg said. Creamy white skin, long blond hair, sky-blue eyes— the description may as well have been of Egg herself.

"Sometimes I have trouble remembering Mom's face exactly or her voice, but I remember her . . . here." I pointed to my heart.

Egg opened the drawer to her nightstand and brought out the beautiful pink pearl earrings she'd been wearing when she arrived. "These were my mother's earbobs. I keep them with me always, to remind me of her." Tears welled up in her eyes.

"Princesses never cry," she said in a strained voice.

I handed her the tissue box. She turned out the light before I had a chance to see if what she said was true.

13.
Ye Spirit and Ye Soccer

We played Ridgeview early Saturday morning. I scored three points, Alisha scored two, but we lost, 7–5. I braced myself for a lecture from Coach but her attention was focused on our goalie, Carly, who had made Ridgeview's job a lot easier.

After our defeat, Alisha and I walked over to the football field, where Pine Glen was battling South High. Dad and Shane were already in the stands, along with the princess. It was her first football game ever, but I don't think she was there to experience contemporary American culture. She was there to see Tino play.

As the Panther football team trounced South 32–7,

Dad enjoyed answering Egg's questions about the game. I, on the other hand, was not amused when she referred to the players as "knights" and called the goalposts the "portcullis." Appallingly, she was fascinated by the cheerleading squad, led by Eden, and she had the mistaken impression that those featherbrains were actually instructing the "knights" on what to do.

After the game, the princess sweetly asked Dad's permission to meet Tino and his friends at the Pizza Palace. Dad hadn't had any experience with a daughter—or a princess—wanting to meet a guy. He hemmed and hawed until Ric materialized right between us in the stands.

"Would you please warn us when you're going to do that?" Dad asked.

"Sorry. I was in kind of a hurry. Just wanted you to know I'm going to be at the Pizza Palace, too. I'll keep an eye on the princess."

"I don't know this Tino guy," Dad said, uneasily.

"He's nice, Dad." I was feeling generous.

"You come, too, Casey," Ric said. "Everybody's going. Alisha will be there."

"Well, if it's a group thing, okay," Dad reluctantly agreed.

"It's not my scene," I told Ric. But then I made the mistake of looking into those emerald eyes and two seconds later I said yes.

Okay, the Pizza Palace wasn't as bad as I'd imagined. Alisha managed to sit next to Taj Oliver, and it wasn't by chance. Tino and Egg were deep in conversation as she explained what she'd learned about the game of football. Apparently, everything she said was hysterically funny—at least to him.

I stayed close to Ric. I felt so different around him—not different, really, because in an odd way, I felt more like myself. More relaxed, more ready to smile or laugh. I had to remind myself that he was only an illusion, a sleight of hand, and a pretty crummy wizard. And I had to remember that if Boricius happened to be successful, I'd probably never see those green eyes again.

Gran and Dad scheduled a conference with Ric for Sunday afternoon. Even though I wasn't invited, I made sure I was right outside the kitchen, sitting in the den with my French book while I eavesdropped.

Dad and Gran were drinking coffee when I saw a poof of purple smoke. I almost gasped when I peeked in and saw Alaric sporting his full wizard getup. Now that I'd seen him as a twenty-first-century teen, he looked silly in his crooked hat and oversize robes.

"We have some concerns about the princess," Gran began. "And as her, uh, representatives, we thought we should discuss them with you."

"That's cool," Ric said, opening the fridge. "Mind if I grab some OJ?"

"Help yourself. But I'm having a problem talking to you," Dad said. "I think it's the hat."

Ric—or rather Alaric—laughed. "Sorry! I've been in Trewellyn and I forgot to switch back."

Dad cleared his throat. "Speaking of Trewellyn, I've been doing some research, but I can't find it in any book or on any map. I met with a history professor over at the university. He's never heard of it either, even though he wrote a big, thick book about medieval times. So tell me, is this some joke or is there a Trewellyn? And where is it? England? France?"

"Neither. Trewellyn is a sovereign nation and the princess's father is the sovereign. Actually it's a small island off the coast of England, surrounded by rough waters. What with the constant fog and the dense cloud of dragon's breath hovering overhead, the mapmaker probably passed it by without notice."

Dad chuckled. "Sounds like a cheery place."

"Casey says the princess speaks fluent French. Why is that?" Gran asked.

"*Oui,*" said the wizard with a chuckle. "Her mother, Queen Fleur, was French. Old alliances, you know. The princess learned French from birth."

"That explains it, doesn't it, Joseph?"

"I guess," Dad reluctantly agreed. "Except the part about the dragon."

"Yoo-hoo! Libby!"

Mrs. Huddleston was back, standing with only a screen door between her and the sight of an authentic wizard!

"I brought over some homemade apple butter," she called.

I could hear the panic in Gran's voice. "Wait! The screen door's locked!"

"No, dear, it's open," Mrs. Huddleston said as she walked right in. I raced into the kitchen to help Alaric. "Ric!" He obviously hadn't fully grasped the situation yet.

"Ah!" he said and quickly made the transition back to Ric. Except for one slight mistake: He was dressed like the twenty-first century but was still wearing a pointy wizard hat!

I madly pointed to my head to signal him while Mrs. Huddleston babbled away. "Joe, I remember how much you liked my apple butter last year, so I told Phil, 'Phil, I'm going to have to make a special batch for Joe.' And here it is."

Thank goodness Dad quickly sized up the situation and placed his tall, husky body between Mrs. Huddleston's field of vision and Ric. Ric removed his hat, and when Dad stepped aside, he looked like a regular teenager again.

"This is Casey's friend, Ric," Gran said.

Ric said hi and Mrs. Huddleston said hi. Then she started to ask about the princess, but she was distracted by the sight of a bright green frog hopping across the kitchen floor.

"Oh, dear! I hope I didn't let that thing in the house," our neighbor said.

We all stared at the frog for a moment, then Dad said, "No, that's Shane's. Must have gotten out of its cage again. Well, thanks for the jam. Hi to Phil."

He herded Mrs. Huddleston toward the back door. "It's apple butter, actually," she protested.

"My favorite." Dad opened the door and practically pushed her out. Once she was gone, we all heaved a sigh of relief. I was glad nobody asked me to leave.

"My, that was a close call," Gran said, sitting down.

"I'll say. Frogs aren't kept in cages, Dad," I told him.

"It's my fault. I always have trouble with these split-second transformations," Ric admitted. "I promise, it won't happen again."

"Speaking of spells, what's going on with that guy—Voracious?" Dad asked pointedly.

"Boricius. Alas, the progress of the spell is slow at best."

"And I have another question." Gran spoke hesitantly. "How do you feel about the princess dating a . . . commoner?" Gran asked.

"Tino? I think he's been good for her highness. Coming here might be the best thing that's ever happened to her."

Well, it wasn't the best thing that ever happened to me, but I had to admit, having Ric around helped. A lot.

On Monday morning, Egg showed up for breakfast wearing a purple kimono, hemmed up short like a jacket. I have no idea where Gran dug that thing up. She wore her short gold skirt with the lace triangle arranged as a neck scarf. And, of course, purple ribbons with her slippers, and streaming ribbons of gold and purple in her hair. Worst of all, she looked way too pleased with herself.

"Don't you think you kind of overdid the school colors thing?" I grumbled over my orange juice.

Egg stroked the sleeve of her kimono. "I will be attending the Spirit Club meeting this afternoon.

Since we will be discussing school spirit, I thought I should wear purple and gold."

"Go, Panthers," I muttered. "What's the point?"

"I was told that the Spirit Club cheers at sporting events as I have done at scores of jousts." Egg sighed. "Of course, I bestowed honors as well."

"Here, you'll be one person in a crowd of people. No one will even notice you."

"*Everyone* notices a princess."

Gran bustled into the kitchen. "Don't you look nice, dear! Aren't those the school colors?"

"Yes. They are also the colors of my father, the king's royal robes," Egg explained.

"What made you want to join the stupid Spirit Club anyway?" I asked.

"Maddy encouraged me."

I almost dropped my toast. "Maddy? The same girl who's got a major crush on Tino?"

Egg frowned. "Maddy and I are friends, Casey."

I shook my head. "Trust me. She's setting you up for something."

"Casey, for once could you please try to think the best of people? You're becoming cynical," Gran scolded.

"I wonder why," I mumbled, shooting a dirty look at the princess. She was too busy retying her scarf to notice.

"Whoo-ee! Way to go, Eglan-tine!" Albert Falutti shouted as the princess walked—no—strutted down the hall that morning. Naturally everybody turned to check her out.

Out of thin air, Ric appeared, flashing a most appealing grin. "Nice sweatshirt, Casey."

"I suppose you're going to join the Spirit Club, too," I said.

"No, I have plenty of spirit already," he replied. "Besides, don't you have soccer practice today?"

"Every day. Why?"

"I thought I might watch. I'm still trying to figure out these modern sports."

"Nobody comes to soccer practice. Your reputation as a cool guy will be ruined."

"Don't worry, no one will see me. Remember?" With that, Ric disappeared completely from view.

"You're supposed to take care of the princess, not me," I reminded the thin air.

Ric appeared again, grinning mischievously.

"Didn't I tell you? I can be in two places at one time. A specialty Boricius taught me."

I was never quite sure whether to believe him.

Just then, the *other* princess, Eden, came walking toward us. She was all smiles and I swear, she even winked at Ric.

"Hi, Ric," she said in a sickeningly sweet voice.

"Hey, Eden, what's up?" he asked.

She reached up and flicked an imaginary piece of lint off his shirt. "You are just the person I was looking for."

I felt nauseous.

"We'd like to get some cool guys in the Spirit Club this year," she said. "Will you come to the meeting today?"

"Sorry. Busy."

"Come on, it won't be too bad. I'll hold your hand if you get scared."

I was trying hard not to barf.

"Nope. I promised I'd watch Casey's soccer practice."

That wiped the silly grin off Eden's face.

"Well, if you change your mind, you know where to find me. You do have my number, don't you?"

"Sure do," Ric answered with a friendly smile as Eden flounced away.

"*I've* got her number, all right," I grumbled.

"Don't worry. So do I." Ric patted my shoulder. That felt nice.

"Don't you want to be in the Spirit Club with all those cute girls?"

"I want the princess to enjoy herself without me looking over her shoulder all the time."

"But you *will* be looking out for her—won't you?"

"And you," he said.

I didn't really need looking after, but I wasn't about to argue with him. Especially after he'd put Eden Endicott in her place, maybe for the first time ever.

True to his word, Ric actually showed up at soccer practice. I was afraid Coach Curson wouldn't be pleased to see him there, so I nervously approached her. "That's my friend up there," I said, pointing to the bleachers. "Is it okay if he watches?"

Coach stared at the stands, shading her eyes with her hand. Finally she said, "What's the joke, Peabody? There's nobody there." She blew her whistle in my ear and practice resumed.

I turned back toward the bleachers, and sure enough, there was Ric waving at me. Then I remembered the Veil of Invisibility. I could see him because he wanted me to. Coach could not.

I guess he wasn't such a bad wizard after all.

14.

Ye Royal Accident

The rest of Egg's second week at Pine Glen Junior High had its ups and downs. Most of the "ups" were for Egg. Most of the "downs" were for me.

On Tuesday, she startled Ms. Speckles and the entire biology class when, at the start of lab, she asked if we would be turning metal into gold. "I'm afraid that only happens in storybooks," the teacher explained.

"Pooh! Any wizard worth his salt can do it," Egg countered. I had to fake a major coughing spell to get the subject changed.

After class, Eden actually came up to the princess and said, "Hi, Egg. Feeling chilly today?"

Egg graced her with a smile and a regal nod.

That same day, our soccer team lost to Fillmore, 4–1. Alisha got our only goal and Coach chewed me out for not passing to Lindsey early in the game. I was glad Ric wasn't there to watch. At least I don't think he was.

On Wednesday, Mrs. Markle gave Egg an A– on her paper about how King Arthur was actually a bad king. The teacher called it "most original." Mine must have been "most mediocre" because I got a B–.

Later that day I saw Sabrina wearing a gold ribbon in her hair. I was pretty sure where she'd gotten her inspiration.

At soccer practice that afternoon, I made sure I passed as often as possible to Lindsey and Heather so Coach wouldn't tear into me. She called me out instead for using poor judgment.

Kiki and Sabrina wore skirts and ribbons in their hair the next day, and M. Dobkins fawned over Egg when she recited some long poem in French. All I got was a C on my French homework. Maybe the princess was right: Royals are superior to commoners, and I was feeling way too common around her.

When Ric showed up at my locker after school, I lit into him. "What are you doing? You should be spending all your time working on getting Princess Know-it-all out of here!" I stuffed my books into my locker.

"Whoa, calm down," Ric said. "I thought you two were getting along, finding things in common."

"We don't have one thing in common. One of us is a normal girl and the other is a royal pain!"

Ric stayed silent.

"Say something," I said after a long wait.

"I'm trying to decide which one of you is the royal pain."

You bet I slammed my locker door—hard.

What I love about soccer: the challenge of moving the ball without my hands, the race across the field after an interception, and the breathtaking feeling when, against all odds, I kick the ball past the opposing keeper. I'm never alone because in my mind, Pelé, David Beckham, and Mia Hamm are playing right alongside me. Most of all, I love the sheer pleasure of running around in the crisp autumn air.

When spring and summer roll around, I've got softball to keep my mind off missing soccer. I love the sounds: the crack of the bat whacking out a solid home run, the swoosh as I slide into a base, the thud as the ball lands in my glove, the sound of the crowd urging me on. Then there are the ghosts: Mantle, Ruth, Maris, and the gutsy women of the All-

American Girls Professional Baseball League, right there on the field with me.

Soccer and softball may only be games, but they're more important to me than almost anything, except my family. I feel as uncomfortable as an itchy sweater when I go to a party, but I feel completely at home when I'm kicking around the soccer field. It's the safest place in the world. Usually. But on that Thursday afternoon, something went terribly wrong. We were in the middle of a simple passing drill and what happened just goes to show you that an athlete can't afford to lose focus. Ever.

I was thinking way too much about Ric. First, I was sorry I'd dumped on him. Second, I wondered if he was watching but invisible. I told myself, "So what? It shouldn't affect my game." After all, he was only a wizard in disguise—right?

Then, as Alisha kicked the ball toward me, I thought I saw a glimpse of red in the stands—Ric in his red sweatshirt? It was a mere flicker, but it made me think there was a glitch in his Veil of Invisibility.

Whatever happened, I was definitely in a Mind Muddle as Alisha passed the ball to me. It bounced up, hitting me right in the eye. That set off a flurry of activity as the girls gathered around me. Coach Curson ordered me to lie down, shouted for ice, and told me not to move. I tried to turn my head to see if

Ric was around, but she wouldn't let me move an inch.

"Could be a concussion," she told Alisha.

"Oh no!" my friend gasped.

"Probably just a shiner," I assured her. Even though it hurt, I managed to keep my other eye open for signs of you-know-who. If he was around, the Veil of Invisibility was working really well.

Coach called Dad, who took me to the emergency room, but all I had was a big, fat black eye. The doctor at the hospital called it a "contusion," which sounded more dramatic.

"Rest tonight and tomorrow," she said.

"It's gonna be a lulu," Dad said with a touch of pride in his voice. "Yessir, that's going to be a shiner to remember."

Gran was waiting at the door—and talking on the phone—when we got home about seven. "She just got home. I'll have her call you later," she said.

I got a much-needed Gran-hug, and Dad guided me to the sofa in the den where Gran had big pillows plumped up, waiting for me. "The phone was ringing off the hook," she said. "I couldn't think about dinner, so I called for a pizza."

The Pain raced in with an ice pack for my eye. "Pizza on a school night!" he exclaimed. Then he leaned in to examine my eye. "Wow, that's awesome!"

That's when I noticed Egg hanging back behind Dad's big chair. She stared at me warily. "'Tis ghastly," she said with a shudder.

I ignored her. "Who was on the phone?" I asked Gran.

"Goodness, poor Alisha's called about ten times. She's feeling guilty. And Coach Curson called and said she'd try again later. Tino called . . ."

"For Egg," I added.

"Well, yes, but he did ask about you. Even Lindsey called. Let's just say you created quite a stir."

The doorbell rang and Shane ran to open it. Pizza always gets him moving.

"Pizza man!" The voice was all too familiar. Ric was at the door, holding two big pizza boxes and a large plastic to-go cup.

"Did you get a job?" Gran asked.

"Nope. I just happened to meet the delivery guy outside," Ric said with a grin. "He said you could pay him later." Yeah, right. I made a mental note to get Ric to teach me his free-pizza spell. "So how's the patient?" he asked.

He marched into the den and leaned in to examine my eye. I took off the ice pack and enjoyed seeing the look of concern on his face.

"Ouch," he said.

"Don't you have a magic spell to take it away?" I asked.

"Naw—too commonplace. I feel guilty that I didn't think to deflect that ball with a spell before it hit you. It never occurred to me that . . ." He stopped, slightly embarrassed.

"That I'd walk right into it?"

He grinned. "To make up for it, I brought you this." He handed me the cup. "Strawberry-banana smoothie. Your favorite, I believe."

It was my favorite, but I was surprised that he'd gone all the way to the Juice Hut to get it for me. No guy had ever done something like that for me.

He gently put the ice pack back on my eye. "Better keep this on," he said softly. My insides did a flip-flop. Those eyes made me feel all melty, but *hold on*—this was Alaric!

"Veggie or pepperoni?" Gran asked, breaking the spell.

"Veggie," I mumbled.

"Leeches," the princess said emphatically. We all turned to stare at her.

"An application of leeches would cleanse the blood. You know that, Alaric."

The Pain made a rude gagging sound.

"Lose the leech talk," Dad said. "Let's talk about something else."

"I've got to do a demonstration speech," Shane announced.

"What's that?" Dad asked.

"I've got to demonstrate how something works and explain the steps," Shane told him.

"I could show you how to build something. Like a birdhouse," Dad volunteered.

Shane wrinkled his nose. "I was thinking Ric could show me how to make Miss Foster disappear."

Ric thoughtfully stroked his chin. "It could be done. . . ."

"Bad idea," Dad said firmly.

"We could make her reappear again right away," Shane protested.

"We'll talk about disappearing people later," Dad said firmly. He turned to Egg. "How was your day, Princess?"

Egg moved toward the pizza. "Fine," she said. "I decided that I will try out to be a cheerleader next week."

I jerked upright, dropping the ice pack into my lap. "Cheerleader?" I fell back onto my pillow and groaned.

"I think it sounds like a nice idea," Gran said. "But don't they already have cheerleaders?"

"They did," the princess explained. "But one of the eighth-grade cheerleaders has moved away."

Ric had a mischievous glint in his eye. "She left the country."

"Rachel Hanrahan," I added. "They're having open tryouts to replace her."

"Switzerland," Ric said mysteriously. "I think that's where they're going. Her father was transferred. Quite unexpected, even to them."

I was afraid to ask him how he knew so much about it, so I turned my attention to the princess. "Why would you want to be a cheerleader? They're just a bunch of egomaniacs who want to be the center of attention. I mean, they don't really contribute to the game or anything."

"Why would you want to be a soccer player?" the princess countered. "Are athletes not just—oh, what is it they say—hot shots who long to be the center of attention? Do you not want to score the most points— more than even your own teammates?"

Egg apparently knew more about sports—and about me—than I thought. "I enjoy the challenge," I explained.

"'Tis good for you! And this will be my challenge. For my whole life, I have had to sit and watch the jousts without showing any emotion. I cannot shout, I cannot clap. For once in my life, I should like to get out there and jump and cheer the competitors on!"

"That's right! Different strokes for different folks," Gran said.

"But you've been to only one football game," I told Egg. "You won't know what to do."

"Yes, I will," the princess replied. "Maddy has offered to teach me."

The ice pack slid off again as I sat upright. "Maddy? Why would the girl you stole Tino away from want to help you? Have you stopped to think about that?"

The princess frowned. "I stole no one! What is she talking about, Alaric?" She turned to Ric, her frown deepening into a scowl. "Must you be in that ridiculous disguise? When I need help, I want the *old* Alaric!"

"Chill out, Your Highness," Ric said soothingly. "You didn't steal Tino. He just likes you more than Maddy. There's no law against that. Certain people like certain people. It doesn't take a wizard to figure that out." He turned to me and winked.

I'm 100 percent sure a guy never winked at me before.

"You know who the cheerleaders are?" I asked. "Eden, for one. And Sabrina and Kiki."

"What's wrong with them?" Egg asked, all innocence.

"They're shallow for one thing. And they laughed at you when you first started school."

Gran tried to intervene. "Casey, if Egg wants to be a cheerleader, it's her decision."

"Well, she won't automatically be chosen just because she's a princess."

"She can win on her own merits." Gran sounded

like Egg's personal cheerleader.

"Why should I not win?" asked Egg. "Has my father, the king, ever withdrawn from battle for fear of losing? I think not."

I gritted my teeth. "It's bad enough living with a princess. But living with a cheerleader . . ." I flopped back on the couch and held the ice to my eye. "It's too much to bear."

"Let us know if we can do anything to help," Gran offered. "Now, Casey, I think you need to go to bed."

Soon, we were in bed with the lights out, and once again Egg wanted to talk.

"Casey . . . is a kiss a terrible thing?" she asked, flicking the light back on.

Tricky question, when you think about it. It depends on the kiss. Duke ambled in and jumped up on Egg's bed as if he was prepared to demonstrate. Duke's slobbery kisses aren't bad, except for that time he ate a whole bowl of tuna salad. But a kiss—boy to girl, lip to lip—how should I know?

"This wouldn't have something to do with Tino, would it?" I asked.

She nodded sheepishly. "Do you think it would ever be all right for Tino to kiss me?"

"Won't Prince Vorland be jealous?"

She shrugged. "I care not."

"He's your fiancé," I reminded her. "You're supposed to marry him."

"I would sooner marry the duke."

That was harsh. "The duke smells bad!" I objected.

"Pah! Everybody smells bad in Trewellyn. The duke, at least, has a heart."

Right on cue, Duke covered her face with big wet kisses.

"It's all right. But Tino *is* a commoner," I reminded her.

The princess sighed. "As you explained, this is a democracy. So, Casey . . . have you ever kissed a boy?"

Another tricky question. A boy named Art kissed me in kindergarten—on a dare. A boy named Zach unexpectedly kissed me in sixth grade, at my first boy-girl party. I wasn't sure those counted as *real* kisses. My heart didn't beat faster. I didn't even get goose bumps.

"Not really," I told her.

"You will," she answered with a knowing smile. Then she flicked off the light.

It took me a long time to get to sleep that night.

15.

Be Ye of Good Cheer

I stayed home on Friday but Coach said if I got a doctor's release, I might be able to play the following Wednesday. By afternoon, my eye was bloodshot and the skin around it was a rainbow of colors. Gorgeous.

Late in the day, after soccer practice, Alisha stopped by with a gigantic balloon bouquet. She must have blown a whole month's allowance on it. When she saw my eye, she flinched.

"Casey, I'm totally sorry I did this to you." She looked so sorry—like one of those sad clown paintings—I could hardly stand it.

"I'm the one who messed up," I assured her. "Stop blaming yourself."

She was blinking back actual tears so I changed the subject.

"What's new at school?" I asked.

"Not much. Everybody's all psyched about the cheerleader thing."

"Egg's trying out," I said glumly.

Alisha didn't seem surprised. "She'll probably make the squad."

"Why do you say that?"

"'Cause she's popular, she's pretty, she's perky. The three *P*s." She giggled.

I didn't add the fourth *P*—princess.

"Anyway, I'd rather have her on the squad than Maddy," Alisha added.

"Maddy probably thinks that if she's a cheerleader, she'll lure Tino away from Egg."

Alisha laughed out loud. "Tino? He only has eyes for your cousin. Trust me."

A car horn blew and Alisha jumped up. "I forgot—my mom's waiting outside! Gotta go!"

After Alisha left, I sat in the den for a while, trying to figure out the real reason Maddy had offered to help Egg. I tried . . . but I couldn't come up with *anything* nice.

I spent the weekend catching up on homework and watching the skin around my eye change from purply pink to dark blue with yellow spots.

The Pain spent the weekend holed up in his room with Ric, working on a demonstration speech. They were acting very hush-hush about the whole thing, which was extremely annoying.

I finally managed to get Ric's attention while, as usual, he was rummaging through the fridge for snacks.

"We've got to talk," I told him.

"Talk away," he answered cheerily as he pulled out a package of salami and another one of cheese. "Cook would faint if she could see all this!" he marveled.

While he was stuffing himself, I said, "Ric, you can't make Shane's teacher disappear for the demonstration speech."

"I can't? Not even for a minute?"

I shook my head firmly. "Nope."

"I already talked Shane out of sending her to Trewellyn for the rest of the term. We were going to use the Veil of Invisibility. It's really minor magic."

"Nope," I told him in no uncertain terms. "I mean it. If that happens, we'll all be banished from Pine Glen."

Ric sighed. "Okay. Just for you, I won't make her disappear."

"Do a regular trick. Make a penny disappear."

He sighed again, rather dramatically. "I don't think Shane will go for that. But Casey . . . do you have any crackers?"

When Ric had finally put together a substantial snack, we sat down at the kitchen table.

"What do you think about this cheerleading thing?" I asked.

"Sounds fine to me."

"Well, what do you think of this Tino thing?"

A few cracker crumbs had settled in one corner of his mouth. "Sounds fine to me," he repeated.

"She was asking about *kissing*." As soon as I said the word, I felt a faint flip-flop in my stomach. "How would her father, the king, feel about that?"

"Don't worry, I'll handle that." Ric chewed on a big bite of salami for a few seconds, staring at me. "You're not really into the guy-girl thing, are you, Casey?"

"I just haven't met a guy I really like."

I started brushing crumbs off the table because I knew I was lying, and I couldn't look Ric straight in his big green eyes.

He was quiet for a while, then amazingly repeated what the princess had said. "You will."

I played the invalid most of the weekend while the princess was at Maddy's house, learning to cheer.

She even put off Tino's invitation to meet at the mall for a movie so she could practice. That was a big relief, considering she probably would have lost it when she saw giant-size actors on the big screen.

"I don't know whether to hope she makes cheerleader or hope she doesn't," I grumbled to Gran.

"Of course you want her to win," said Gran. "After all, she's your cousin."

"Gran!" I whined, and she burst out laughing.

"I know it's weird, but I really do think of her as a granddaughter. I've grown rather fond of her, haven't you?"

"Fond?" I thought it over. "No, but I've gotten used to her. Of course, I've gotten used to this black eye, too."

Gran chuckled. "I get your point, dear. More ice for your eye?"

"It doesn't seem to be doing any good."

"Well, then how about my no-fail treatment for all that ails you?" she asked with her eyes twinkling.

"Double-hot-chocolate with extra marshmallows? You're on!" I exclaimed.

Gran always knows how to turn a bad mood inside out.

Late on Sunday afternoon, Egg returned from her weekend at Maddy's. Her cheeks were unusually rosy and she was practically bursting with excitement.

"How did it go?" Gran asked.

"'Twas brilliant!" Egg gushed. "Maddy was most awesomely helpful. She taught me all the secrets of cheerleading."

Egg moved in closer to examine my eye. "'Tis still most abysmal, your eye. You surely cannot go to school like that."

I sighed. "If I want to play on Wednesday, I've got to get back to practice."

"She'll be fine, Your Highness," Gran assured her. "Now, why don't you show us what you learned?"

The princess's eyes were dancing. "Do you really want to see?"

"Sure," Gran said. "Don't you, Casey?"

"I wouldn't miss it for the world," I answered, settling back on the couch.

The princess stood in the center of the den and began a mindless chant that went something like this:

> We're the Panthers of Pine Glen.
> Let us tell you once again!
> Panthers, Panthers, that's our name.
> We are masters of the game!

She was quite a sight to see. She flapped her arms like a limp chicken, jumped up a whopping three inches, then ended with her arms flung out and one knee bent. Her voice sounded high, shrill, and nasal.

Duke crawled under the sofa. I was ready to join him.

Gran cleared her throat. "That was, uh, interesting. What do you think, Casey?"

"Is that what Maddy taught you?" I asked.

"Yes. We have worked on it for two whole days," she answered proudly.

"I could hardly hear you," I observed.

"Maddy says one must not yell too loudly or one will be disqualified," Egg explained.

Uh-oh. "You didn't jump very high," I said gently.

"Maddy said that most of the cheerleaders cannot jump high and if you outdo them, you shall be automatically disqualified."

I was boiling inside. Egg may have faults—okay, a lot of them—but she didn't deserve this kind of treatment. If I didn't help Egg, Maddy's nasty plan to make her a lousy cheerleader would succeed. If I did help Egg, and she made cheerleader, she'd win fair and square. My decision wasn't that difficult.

"Princess—I think you've been had," I said.

Gran nodded. "I agree."

Egg blinked several times. She looked totally confused. "*Had?* What is this *had?*"

"Duped. Conned. Hoodwinked. Hornswoggled," Gran explained.

Egg was still blinking.

"She means Maddy tried to trick you into being a *bad* cheerleader," I explained. "She taught you all the wrong things so you'd lose."

Egg sunk down onto the sofa. Duke crawled out and rested his chin on her knee.

"Why?"

I chanted in my best cheerleader imitation:

> *T-I-N-O*
> *Maddy's jealous, don't you know?*

The princess covered her eyes. "You mean I was terrible?"

"Sorry to say, honey," Gran said.

Egg looked heartbroken. "Father would be so disappointed!"

Gran jumped up, surprisingly spry. "You're not giving up without a fight, are you?" she challenged the princess. "You are your father's daughter, remember?"

I thought I saw Egg's mouth quiver. Gran kept talking. "I never told you girls, but I was a cheerleader back in college, and I still remember a thing or two."

I gasped. "You weren't!"

"I was," Gran answered with a gleam in her eye. "I still have a few secrets left. We had male cheer-leaders, too. They'd pick us girls up and throw us in the air."

This time Egg gasped. "Did they catch you again?"

Gran giggled. "Most of the time. Anyway, let's see how much I remember."

My grandmother seemed smaller and younger as she stood in the middle of the floor, swinging her arms.

Boom-a-lacka! Boom-a-lacka!
Use your might!
Boom-a-lacka! Boom-a-lacka!
Fight-fight-fight!

Then she managed an impressive leap for a woman of her age.

Go . . . Bulldogs!

She landed hard and seemed kind of dazed. I rushed to her side.

"Gran, are you all right?"

"I think my boom-boom is a-lacking these days," she said as I helped her to the couch. "Sorry,

Princess. Guess I can't be of much help to you."

"Please don't hurt yourself, Gran," Egg said. It was the first time I heard her call my grandmother "Gran." I felt a pang when she said it. "Cheerleading is not as important as your well-being," she continued.

The girl had a heart after all.

"There's no reason to give up," I said. "The try-outs aren't until Wednesday afternoon! Remember how fast you learned to run?"

I noticed a smile tugging at the corners of Gran's mouth.

"How shall I learn?" Egg asked.

"Oh, I'll teach you," I said grudgingly. "I may not like cheerleaders, but that doesn't mean I can't do what they do."

"That's a generous offer, Casey," Gran said. "Don't you think so, Princess?"

"If you do that, I shall present you with a royal commission!" Egg promised.

"Don't do me any favors. Just show Maddy you can't push a Peabody around."

"Well said!" Gran rubbed her hands together. "Let's get to work!"

I'm embarrassed to admit that I've been analyzing those annoying cheerleaders for years. I try hard to ignore them but it's pretty difficult, especially when they block my view of the game. Half of them wouldn't know a touchdown from a touch-up on their bleached roots. They're afraid of getting their hair messed up, and they're always pulling mirrors out of their pockets to check their makeup. Okay, not everyone. Desiree Washington doesn't even wear makeup. She's an amazing gymnast. And Lillian Chang is an awesome dancer who truly deserves to be a cheerleader, unlike Princess Eden and her ladies-in-waiting.

"Remember, you're there to *move* people," I told her. "You're a leader."

Egg stood up straight and tall. "Like my father, the king!"

"Exactly! If you were leading the crowd at a joust, would you yell softly and do some kind of a wimpy jump?" I asked.

"Never!" Egg said, shocked at the thought of it.

"*You're* in charge. The crowd is counting on you. And remember this: Anything worth doing is worth getting your hair messed up for," I told her.

"Mercy," Gran murmured. "Those are words to live by!"

"Is there a required routine or do you get to pick your own?" I asked.

"Maddy says we must plan our own two-minute routines."

"Good! Now, let me show you some *real* cheer-leading moves."

I did gymnastics when I was a kid and I knew Egg would get points for any tumbling from cartwheels to backflips. I demonstrated my first cartwheel and Egg's eyes grew wide.

"But cheerleaders wear such tiny skirts!"

Once I assured her that those little skirts had little shorts sewn inside, she was ready for the basics. Gran quietly disappeared, leaving me on my own.

I'm no track star but I've cleared my share of high hurdles so it wasn't much of a leap to figure out how to do cheerleading jumps. Teaching Egg how to do them was a different story, though.

"The judges have a scorecard, so you get points for doing different jumps, the harder the better. You also earn points for stuff like how you look, how loud you cheer, and how high you score in perkiness."

"What is 'perkiness'?" Egg asked.

"You know. This." I did my best imitation of a bubbly elf, kind of like Maddy.

Egg shook her head. "Princesses are not perky. We are regal." She straightened her spine, threw back her shoulders, lifted her chin.

I doubted they gave points for regal, but who knows? "Whatever. Anyway, let's see you jump."

Egg demonstrated with a pathetic hop.

"That was more of a lurch," I told her. "You've got to launch yourself like a rocket."

Egg wrinkled her nose. "Rocket? What is that?"

"Like a spaceship. You know. *Star Wars*?"

Right on cue, a huge swirl of purple smoke poured out of the fireplace. When it cleared, Ric was standing on the hearth like a Santa Claus with sparkling green eyes and an irresistible grin.

"Sorry I'm late."

"It's about time you helped out," the princess scolded him. "What is this rocket?"

"You know, it sends you straight up . . . like a catapult."

The princess stamped her foot impatiently. "Just teach me to jump like a cheerleader."

"Is that a command?" he asked.

"No," Egg admitted quietly. "I am merely asking for your help."

The princess was becoming so respectful, pretty soon she'd learn to say "please."

"No magic," I said firmly. "I'll turn her in if you use magic. It's cheating."

"What is the point of having a wizard?" The princess sounded quite exasperated.

"Chill. I have no intention of using magic," Ric replied.

"Which reminds me, we wouldn't be doing this at all if you hadn't made Rachel Hanrahan move to Switzerland." I pointed an accusing finger at his chest. "You did do that, didn't you?"

Ric looked completely innocent. "Hey, I'm a wizard, but I can't control multinational corporations."

"Pooh. Of course he can," the princess argued.

The discussion ended when Gran bustled back into the den, waving a sheaf of papers. "Look what I found on the Internet. Cheerleading lessons complete with instructions and illustrations."

Ric and I studied them, then began the lessons for real. First, we had to get Egg to jump. *Really* jump.

Then, we worked on getting her to jump high enough to tuck her legs up into her chest, with her arms extended.

"Think of it as levitation," Ric suggested. "Watch."

He took a giant leap and when he reached his natural high point, he floated up to the peak of the vaulted ceiling.

"Watch your head!" Gran warned.

Ric stopped just before he hit the ceiling and tucked his legs up into his chest, arms spread out. He remained there, hovering in the air.

"Watch out, Eden," I said. "Ric's got my vote."

Egg's blue eyes turned dark. "Casey said no magic!"

Ric obediently floated back down. "I was only giving you something to aim for."

Egg tried again and she showed real improvement, though she was in no danger of hitting the ceiling.

After a while, Shane wandered in. "Isn't anybody hungry?" he asked in a whiny voice. That was his subtle way of saying that somebody should be cooking dinner. When nobody budged, Shane disappeared into the kitchen and Duke followed.

"Feed Duke while you're in there," Gran called after him.

We moved on to the pike, where you bend your body in half, with both legs straight out and toes pointed. After a few attempts—and no magic—the princess got the hang of it.

Dad wandered in. "Boy, I had no idea how late it was getting," he said, staring at his watch. That was *his* subtle way of saying somebody should be cooking dinner. No one answered, so he trudged into the kitchen.

"Make sure Shane fed Duke," Gran called after him.

We worked on the jumps awhile longer, until Dad came in carrying a big plate of sandwiches. Shane followed with a bag of chips.

"Dinner is served," Dad proudly announced. "Toasted cheese sandwiches."

"And chips," Shane added.

"I'm impressed," said Gran. "Is there any chance of getting a vegetable in there somewhere?"

Dad stared down at his plate. "Potatoes are vegetables, aren't they? As in potato chips?"

The princess wasn't interested in the food but Ric eagerly grabbed a sandwich. "I've got to tell Cook about these."

Duke sat up and begged for something to eat.

"You never change, Duke," the princess chuckled. "Always looking for a handout."

"Didn't anyone feed him?" Gran asked.

Dad excused himself and called Duke into the kitchen.

After everyone—including Duke—had eaten, the princess, Ric, and I moved on to cartwheels, even though Gran thought we should wait until dinner digested.

"No time," I told her.

Cartwheels were no problem for me, but it took Ric and Egg a while to do them gracefully. Before long, the three of us were making circles around the room.

Around ten thirty, Gran said, "You're making me

dizzy. I'm going to bed and I suggest you do the same."

I yawned, Ric's eyelids drooped, and we said good night as well.

When I woke up some time after midnight, Egg's bed was still empty.

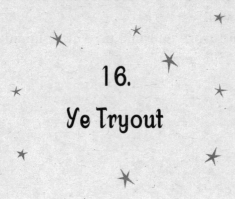

16.
Ye Tryout

"Are you going to school—like that?" the princess asked at breakfast on Monday.

"If you're referring to my eye, it's pretty hard to go to school without it."

"'Tis such a thing as paint. Makeup, as you say."

"I suggested that," Gran said. "She won't wear it."

The princess stared at me for an uncomfortably long time. "Might I try something?"

"No makeup." I was firm.

"'Tis not." She reached over and pulled out the elastic band that held my hair into a tight ponytail.

I tensed up. "You're going to cover my face with my hair?"

"Just your eye." She fooled around with my hair for a while, arranging it with her fingers. Then she told me to look in the mirror.

I never wear my hair down. It's too much trouble and too fussy for sports. But the way the princess fixed it, a little wave came down across my forehead, covering a good portion of the purple ring around my eye.

"It does help a little," I admitted, staring at the unfamiliar image before me.

"You look most comely," the princess said.

I'm not sure why, but I decided to go with it. After all, I may be the only girl on the planet whose hair-dresser is a real live princess.

Maddy was waiting at Egg's locker when we got to school. "Did you practice everything I taught you?" she asked in her chipmunk voice.

"Yes, I practiced a lot," answered the princess. She didn't mention that she practiced what *I* taught her.

Egg's outfit of the day included gold ribbons around her legs, and a short, pale-green dress with gold braid crisscrossed above the waist. Green and gold barrettes pulled back her hair. She got plenty of attention, but now instead of gawking and giggling, people said things like "Egg, you *rule!*" (If they only knew.) Or "That outfit *rocks!*" I even heard Noah say, "You look *chilly*, Egg!"

Actually I got my share of compliments about my hair. Funny how people notice a small change like that. Funny how the attention didn't bother me as much as I'd imagined.

Even Ric said I ought to wear my hair like that more often. I quickly told him I was just covering up the black eye, but I was a little worried that I was falling under the spell of the princess like everyone else.

For the next few days, Egg was serene and imperturbable, correcting her teachers, showing off her French, and letting Tino follow her around like an adoring puppy. At home, we didn't see much of her because she spent all her spare time in the garage, which she insisted on calling the "stable." She also insisted on being there alone.

"I have to do it all on my own," she said when I offered to help. "Like my father, the king."

I stopped myself from pointing out that for her father, the king, "on his own" meant with the help of his own personal army, wizard, mathematician, and jester.

On Tuesday, the doctor gave me the okay to return to soccer, but Coach Curson went easy on me at practice. The game on Wednesday was against Newton, a team we traditionally crushed, so she wasn't that worried.

Wednesday was also the day of cheerleading try-outs. Egg didn't seem nervous, but the rest of us Peabodys were, even Gran. I was so edgy, I snapped at Ric when I found him chasing a lizard near my locker on Wednesday morning.

"Can't you keep those things under control?"

"I'm a wizard, not a zookeeper," he said. "Are you going to tryouts this afternoon?"

"I have a game. I'll have to see how long it lasts." I slammed my locker door. "Promise me you're not going to use magic to make her win."

Ric tucked the lizard back in his backpack. "Is that a command? You're sounding more and more like the princess."

My cheeks were hot. "I am not! Just promise me—no magic."

Ric crossed his heart. "I promise. If she succeeds, it will be because of *her* magic, not mine."

Coach Curson let me play only half the game against Newton, even though my eye had faded to light gray with yellow polka dots. We still trounced them, 5–0. Alisha scored three points. I scored two.

Dad was at my game, but Gran and Shane were in the gym, watching the tryouts. "I'd like to catch the tail end of tryouts," Dad said afterward, which didn't leave me much choice.

Things were in full swing when we got to the gym. Technically, tryouts were only open to Spirit Club members and the judges, but there's always an audience in the bleachers.

Gran patted the bench next to her, and Dad and I quietly slid into place. Seated at long tables on the sidelines were the assistant principal, Mrs. Temple, Mr. Jablonski, Coach Raging Rodgers, M. Dobkins, and a counselor named Mrs. Gould. Then there were the student body president, the honor society president, and the cheerleading squad. They all had sheets of paper in front of them and pencils poised for grading the hopefuls.

I looked around and spotted Ric sitting a few rows back. When he waved, I gave him a stern look and managed to mouth the words, "No magic." He grinned and waved again.

A girl named Rosie was halfway through her audition as we sat down. She had pale thin hair and a pale thin voice and was shaky on her split. As soon as she finished, the judges wrote their decisions in a hurry. I didn't think the verdict was going to be good for Rosie.

Denise Ochoa was next. She was great at swinging her hips and shaking her pom-poms but her voice cracked a couple of times and she jumped about as high as Gran could. Nope, I'm pretty sure Gran could out-boom-a-lack her.

Afterward, the judges concentrated on their ballots for a few minutes. I noticed Eden roll her eyes at Sabrina before they wrote their scores. Denise was definitely *not* going to be the new cheerleader.

Next up was Maddy. She was decent cheerleader material with that fixed smile on her face and the stiff, prepackaged positioning of her arms and legs. She had a good jump and her piercing voice really carried. She certainly didn't follow the advice she had given Egg. She possessed the three *P*s, and when she finished, Eden looked at Sabrina and gave a nod. Maybe Maddy had a chance.

Then they called the next name. Eglantine Peabody.

My throat tightened and my mouth felt dry. I was either coming down with the flu or I was nervous for the princess.

Gran gripped my arm. "This is it," she whispered loudly. "Cross your fingers."

Standing as straight as a ballet dancer, Egg regally strode out to the center of the gym floor. Her hair, which had been flowing in the morning, was entirely different now. She had two sections of hair braided starting at her temples. The braids were pulled back and held with a barrette. The rest of her golden hair was loose but instead of its usual soft curls, it was straight as an arrow. There wasn't a ribbon in sight. This was one serious princess.

She wore a short togalike dress in deep purple with a gold sash. Instead of the usual slippers and ribbons on her feet, she wore—I kid you not—Doc Martens and pale pink tights.

Gran's elbow poked at my ribs. "You won't believe the deal I got on those boots."

"*I* want a pair," I whispered back.

Rather than nervously launching right into a cheer like the other girls, Egg had the guts to stand and wait for the gym to quiet down. Then she raised one arm and pointed to the crowd, her finger moving from right to left, slowly turning in a half circle, fixing the audience in her riveting gaze. Her voice rang out strong and clear. "As your leader, I command you to cheer!"

Now I was the one gripping Gran's arm.

Egg began to clap out a cheerleader's rhythm. *Clap, clap, clap-clap-clap. Clap, clap, clap-clap-clap.*

"Clap!" she shouted in her most commanding voice as she continued. "Clap!"

From the crowd, a smattering of halfhearted

clapping began. Egg was unfazed.

"Clap! I command you, clap!"

The clapping built as the spectators obediently joined in. Once the level of noise had risen, Egg began to chant. "Pan-thers! Pan-thers! Pan-thers!"

Even Gran and Shane joined in, but I was too mesmerized to clap. I was trying to figure out what was coming next.

Once the clapping and the shout of "Panthers!" gained momentum, Egg began stomping her feet in the same rhythm. *Stomp, stomp, stomp-stomp-stomp! Stomp, stomp, stomp-stomp-stomp!*

"Stomp! I command you!"

It didn't take long for the stomping to build to a thunderous roar. I stayed silent, though, because I was worried that the crowd would never be able to hear Egg cheer. Never underestimate a princess.

She segued into a Riverdance kind of stomp, twirling in a circle as the clapping, the stomping, and the cry of "Pan-thers!" continued. A couple of people in the stands whistled. Someone shouted, "Go, Egg!" I even heard someone yell, "Chilly!"

Next, against this frenzy she had created, Egg began a traditional cheer that seemed bigger and more important because of the excitement she had created.

"Go Panthers! Go fight! Go Panthers! Go win!"

This time she didn't have to command the crowd to cheer along.

"Go Panthers!" As if bouncing off an invisible trampoline, she jumped a good three feet off the ground and touched her toes with her outstretched hands, then landed lightly on both feet. I noticed that Egg had taken the trouble to wear a pair of pale purple shorts under her toga. A princess doesn't take chances.

"Go fight!" Again, she rose effortlessly into a high jump, with both legs bent to one side. Her landing was impeccable.

I glanced back at Ric. He was leaning back against the empty bench behind him, completely relaxed. He wasn't doing anything more magical than enjoying the show.

"Go Panthers!" The princess spread her arms out wide and jumped up with her knees tucked up under her chest.

The crowd was practically insane with excitement but the princess was just getting warmed up. Her voice could be heard above the roar. "Go, fight, win! Go, fight, win! Go Panthers!"

She did a circle of cartwheels—four, I think— ending in a full split, arms raised high in a victory V.

"I command it!"

To say the crowd went wild is such a cliché, but

it's no exaggeration. All the spectators were on their feet, cheering. The judges were on their feet cheering, too, except for Eden, Sabrina, and Kiki, who looked a little shaken by Egg's performance.

The princess gave her audience a dainty curtsy and hurried off to the sidelines.

We Peabodys all jumped up and down. "She did it!" Gran shouted. "You taught her well!"

"Believe me," I answered truthfully, "I didn't teach her any of that."

I watched the judges, who were sitting again and writing furiously. Eden, Sabrina, and Kiki were writing, too, but they looked smaller and paler than before.

Later, you could hardly see Egg for the circle of admirers gathered around her. In true princess style, she serenely thanked them. Denise and the others who'd tried out stood on the sidelines, looking miserable. Maddy simply slinked away. I was too amazed at what I'd seen to feel sorry for them. Hard as it was to admit, I was feeling *proud*.

During dinner, Egg got the call from Mrs. Temple, to tell her that, of course, she was selected as the new eighth-grade cheerleader. Gran was so excited, I thought she was going to cartwheel across the room.

The princess, on the other hand, was quite subdued.

"Aren't you happy?" Dad asked.

"Of course," Egg answered. "However, I am not surprised."

Here I was feeling happy for her and she has to pull her sense-of-entitlement routine. I was ready to growl at her when she continued.

"I could not have done it without Casey," Egg said.

It was nice of her, I guess, but I felt as if she was patting me on the head like Duke.

"At least you got back at that snake, Maddy," I said, after a pause.

"She is of little consequence to me," Egg replied. "In fact, I plan to pardon her."

Personally, I would have sent her to the dungeon for a long time.

"Now you can cheer for your *boyfriend*," Shane said, being as great a pain as ever.

"Actually, I am eagerly anticipating cheering for Casey at the next soccer game," Egg replied.

Shane choked and came dangerously close to squirting milk out of his nose. "Soccer game? Cheerleaders don't cheer at soccer games! *Girls* don't cheer for *girls*."

The princess's beautiful wide eyes opened even wider. "Of course they do. The role of the cheerleader is to cheer the athletic teams of Pine Glen on to victory. That's what they said at Spirit Club."

"Boys' teams," I explained. "They only cheer for football and boys' basketball."

"Not all the boys' teams. The cheerleaders don't cheer for boys' baseball," Dad observed.

"That's true," said Gran. "Maybe they're worn out by spring."

Egg stood up, rising to her full, regal height. "Are you saying that cheerleaders cheer for boys' sports but not girls' sports?"

We all looked puzzled. "I never thought of it before, but that's true," I admitted. "Not many people even come to the girls' soccer games. Just parents, mostly."

Familiar storm clouds were gathering in Egg's eyes. "You told me that in this country, everyone is treated equally. And now, you tell me this!"

Dad seemed embarrassed. "In theory, everyone in this country is equal, under the law. But I don't think you could say that everyone is treated equally across the board."

"This is what comes of not having a king!" Egg haughtily shook her head and strode away from the table.

We all sat in silence for a moment until The Pain said, "She didn't ask to be excused."

Gran stared at Egg's empty place at the table. "I'm going to let it pass this time. All right with you, Joseph?"

Dad glumly nodded. "Yep."

When I went to my room to do homework, Egg was on her bed, a book spread across her legs, staring into space.

"Aren't you going to call Tino and tell him the good news?" I asked.

She slammed the book shut. "I am furious."

I plopped down on my bed. "You mean about that equality thing?"

"I feel as if I have been made a fool of. I was misled into believing everyone was equal in this country! I shall resign at once!"

I don't know why, but I hated the idea of her quitting after she'd done such a good job. "Quit? You've reached the heights! You're a cheerleader—enjoy it!"

Egg wrinkled her nose. "Why? Is it supposed to be fun?"

"Sure. You get to wear the uniform, ride the bus with the team to away games . . ."

"With Tino?" She brightened up at that.

I nodded. "Everyone admires a cheerleader. It's

sort of like being a princess."

I guess I said the right thing because she relaxed and put on her tiara.

But something else was nagging at me.

"You know, you do have to keep up your grades to stay on the squad," I told her.

"That shall not be a problem," she answered with complete confidence.

"Isn't English a problem? Let's face it. Your writing is a little old-fashioned."

"Well, my grade was a C until that essay on King Arthur last week. I got an A, which brought my grade up to a B."

"Okay. And I know you're doing well in French. But history? Have you finally admitted the earth isn't flat?"

The princess stuck her royal nose in the air. "Of course not. Ric explained that I was to *pretend* to believe the teacher, the way Father makes me pretend to like the commoners when I go to town. You know, smile and wave, like that."

Since smiling, waving, and pretending are so *not* me, I moved on to math.

"Ah, yes. Well, Ms. Espinoza realizes that I am a *tad* behind the rest of the class and has been giving me different homework and quizzes. I'm doing quite well."

"You mean, she gives you baby math?"

Egg bristled at the word "baby." "'Tis only fair. I cannot be expected to do work that I have not been prepared for. Before you even ask, I am doing fine in biology. The lab experiments remind me of Alaric's dear potions—a little tamer, perhaps. And I am getting straight A's in French, chorus, and P.E. Actually my average is higher than most of the other cheerleaders. Don't worry, Casey. I shall not be eliminated from the squad *if* I choose to remain."

"Good." I was surprised and relieved.

"I do have a question. What is this 'homecoming' they all talk about?" she asked.

I explained that homecoming is the weekend of the big football game against our rivals, Hillside. There's a pep rally on Friday night, the game on Saturday afternoon, and a dance that night.

Egg got a faraway look in her eyes as she smoothed imaginary wrinkles from her skirt. "Ah, the dance! Tino has already asked me. Will you be in attendance?"

"I haven't decided," I mumbled as I got up to leave.

There was a knock. "Tino's on the phone," Dad said.

Egg was out the door so fast, her tiara almost fell off.

17.

Ye Strange Substitute

For the next few days, a crowd of well-wishers hung around the princess—squealing over her, hugging her, acting like her best friends. Even Eden and her entourage joined in. The icing on the cake was when Maddy showed up at school with blue ribbons laced up around her legs. She was hardly alone. Ribbon streamers, short skirts, ballet slippers, and gold braid were becoming common in the halls of Pine Glen Junior High. Kids started saying "chilly" instead of "cool," and adding "I command you" to just about every sentence.

When I pointed out the Eglantine phenomenon sweeping the school, the princess replied, "I told you, Casey, be yourself and people will accept you."

Right.

I didn't see much of her that week. She spent most of her time with the cheerleading squad practicing for Saturday's game. I even heard her mumble "Go team" in her sleep one night.

By game time on Saturday, the crowd was more excited about Egg's cheerleading debut than they were about the game. The princess's influence could not be denied. After all, the cheerleaders wore purple and gold streamers in their hair. When it came time for the first cheer, Eden, Sabrina, and Kiki stepped forward and began clap-clap-clapping.

Clap, clap, clap-clap-clap. "Go Panthers!" they yelled.

Clap, clap, clap-clap-clap. "Go fight!"

They gamely kept at it for a few more rounds of clapping, but the crowd just wasn't responding.

"We want Egg!" an anonymous voice called out.

"We want Egg! We want Egg!" a chorus of voices joined in.

Eden, Sabrina, and Kiki turned back to the other cheerleaders, who joined them in clapping. Even Egg.

"We want Egg! We want Egg!" The spectators were stomping their feet now, completely drowning out the puny little squawks of Eden and her friends, who gamely kept clap-clap-clapping as they backed away from the stands.

"WE WANT EGG!" the crowd roared.

It was almost sad to see Eden's perky smile fade, her chin drop, her shoulders slump. I say *almost* because I was actually smiling big-time and so were the rest of the Peabodys. Eden whispered something in the princess's ear and it barely took Egg a second to respond. She stepped in front of the other cheerleaders and raised both hands. Instantly the crowd grew quiet. It was thrilling.

The princess stepped forward and shouted, "I command you to *cheer*!"

The crowd responded with such a ruckus, I saw The Pain cover his ears. Soon, Egg had the crowd clap-clap-clapping along with her, and in a truly noble gesture, she beckoned the other cheerleaders to stand next to her and cheer along.

Finally the game began. I was half expecting the coaches to consult the princess before starting. Egg made a superb cheerleader, regal yet enthusiastic— especially whenever Tino made a play. The Panthers won, and I have no doubt that the cheering crowd helped. I cheered, too, with Ric at my side, yelling his lungs out.

Weird.

With Ric's urging, Dad agreed that it would be fine for Egg to go out with Tino and some friends later that night to celebrate. I secretly hoped that Ric would suggest we go to the Pizza Palace again, too, but he wanted to help Shane finalize his demonstration speech . . . at least that's what he said. Alisha and Taj (who acted like a *couple* now—*whoa!*) asked me to come with them. I didn't want to feel like a fifth wheel, so I gave them an excuse and ran a couple of miles instead.

Sigh.

While Egg got ready to go out, Gran made Shane practice his speech. I would have felt sorry for him except I had had to do the same thing back in sixth grade. You'd have thought The Pain would have been happy to perform a magic trick with the help of a real wizard. Instead, he was wearing the same gloomy expression Duke gets when he's about to get a bath.

"Why do I have to show you?" he asked as we all gathered around the kitchen table.

"Because it's a good way to practice. And because we'd like to see it," Gran said.

"Come on, Shane," Ric encouraged him. "Wizards like to show off their magic."

Shane sighed dramatically and laid out his props: note cards, a coin, and a wand.

"Is that a real wand?" Dad asked.

"I wanted to borrow Alaric's real wand but he wouldn't let me," Shane complained.

"Thank goodness for that. We've had enough magical accidents around here," Gran said.

"I loaned Shane my junior wand," Ric explained. "The one I used when I was a young apprentice. It has only a little bit of magical power."

I don't think that made Gran feel much better.

"It's a baby wand." Shane sounded bitter. "For babies."

"For young wizards-in-training," Ric corrected him. "Like you."

Shane brightened a bit and he began his speech. The idea—as Shane explained it—was to distract the audience by looking at the wand as if you were going to pick it up. You then sneakily switched the coins while no one was paying attention. In other words, the trick would only work with a pretty dumb audience—at least that's how I saw it. But still, everyone applauded, *except* the princess.

"Oh really, Alaric," she chided him. "You could do better than that! How about the Bucket-of-Gold trick?"

Ric shifted nervously. "I don't think they want real magic."

"*I* do," Shane said.

"Who would not love to see thousands of gold

coins tumbling out of thin air into an empty bucket?" the princess insisted.

"I wouldn't mind seeing that myself," Dad joked. "I've got a bucket out in the garage."

"Joseph, we will not have that kind of magic in this house," Gran said firmly. "Ric is right, Your Highness. I'm nervous about Shane using a real magic wand."

The princess sighed loudly. "Magic 'tis not everything. Why, Jove, our royal jester, knew nothing of magic, yet see what he taught me."

The princess darted into the kitchen and returned almost immediately with three apples . . . and a knife.

"Shane. Behold!"

With that, the princess stuck the knife in her gold braid belt and proceeded to start juggling the three apples in a perfect circle . . . throwing them higher and higher with each turn. It was better than anything I'd seen at the circus . . . at the county fair . . . on TV, and she made it look so effortless. We were all *ooh*ing and *ahh*ing, but we stopped when, mid-juggle and without missing a beat, the princess whipped the knife out of her belt, held it straight up, and managed to catch one—then two—then three apples on its point!

We clapped, we cheered, we were completely amazed. All except Ric, who'd turned kind of pale.

The Pain jumped up and down like a four-year-old. "Teach me! Teach me!" he begged.

"Of course. 'Tis so easy."

"No knives at school," Gran reminded Shane. The princess looked disappointed but we all assured her that the juggling alone would assure Shane an A on his speech.

Just about then, Tino arrived and we insisted that she repeat the juggling routine for him. He was completely speechless.

"Where'd you learn that?" he asked when he finally got over his initial shock.

"Our jester," Egg began.

"Our *uncle* Jester," I quickly interrupted. "Jester Peabody. What a character!" My fake giggle didn't sound too convincing but no one noticed.

"Teach me now," Shane pleaded with her.

"Yeah, me too," Tino said.

By the time Egg and Tino left, Shane knew how to juggle, and Gran was left with enough smashed apples to make a gallon of homemade applesauce.

The downside: Ric was gloomy the rest of the evening. "It wasn't magic at all, just a jester's little trick," he complained. He felt a little better after I made him some popcorn. That was a trick he couldn't get enough of.

I expected Egg to wake up with a sunny disposition after her night out with Tino. Instead, she was in one of her foul-weather moods.

"I wish my father, the king, could be here to sort this out for me," she complained at breakfast.

I tried to picture the king making toast in our kitchen, dipping his long sleeves in the jam.

"Sort out what, dear?" Gran asked as she filled our juice glasses.

"This cheerleading catastrophe! Last night at the party, when I suggested to Eden that we cheer at the girls' soccer games, she laughed as if it were a jest— a common joke! And when I explained to her that this land was a democracy, she laughed even harder!"

"Really, Egg, I don't even want cheerleaders at my soccer games. Don't worry about it," I told her.

"Is it not the principle of the matter? 'Tis it not what King Arthur had in mind when he devised the Round Table, which we studied in school?"

"Well, what are you going to do about it?" Gran asked, sounding feisty.

Egg replied confidently. "I shall cheer at the game myself. When do you next play, Casey?"

"Tuesday. But you really don't have to . . ."

"Rest assured there will be *one* cheerleader in attendance."

"Great," I said, not meaning it at all.

Maybe I should have tried to discourage her, but let's face it, the girl could impale three airborne apples on one knife. She was pretty unstoppable.

When I walked into English class on Tuesday, we had a substitute, which should have meant it was going to be an easy day. But this guy looked like a combination of Attila the Hun and Darth Vader, with a huge head looming over powerful shoulders. A long white scarf hung loosely around his neck and he wore a jacket of deep purple. He introduced himself as Mr. Wise.

Mr. Wise had an over-the-top style, like a hammy Shakespearean actor. He began class by waving a big ruler in the air, rapping it hard on the desk, and roaring, "Pupils!" The room quickly grew silent as he began to write on the board in broad strokes. "Please observe these words, which I chanced to hear in the hallway of this so-called institution of higher learning this very morning."

Egg had a puzzled expression on her face and I had a kind of funny feeling in the pit of my stomach.

Mr. Wise finished writing and pointed to the sentence on the board. "Me and him will be there Saturday night," he read. "Would someone like to explain what is incorrect about that sentence?"

Well, it didn't sound good, but Pine Glen students aren't usually anxious to go out on a limb. No hands were raised, so Mr. Wise started calling on people. "Mr. Chung, would you enlighten us?"

Noah shrugged his shoulders. "I don't know. Maybe 'Him and I will be there?'"

"That is one hundred percent *in*correct," Mr. Wise announced. "How about you, Miss Ames?"

Maddy fidgeted with her hair and squeaked, "I and him?"

"I and him will be there Saturday night," the teacher said. "Shockingly *in*correct. How about you, Your Maj—Miss Peabody?"

Egg looked as puzzled as I felt. "Miss *Eglantine* Peabody," Mr. Wise said.

With an air of supreme confidence, Egg replied, "*We* shall be there Saturday night."

Mr. Wise sadly shook his head. "Disappointingly you've missed the entire point."

Aceman's hand shot up. Mr. Wise unwisely called on him. "Yes, Mr. Paceman?"

"I'm not gonna be there Saturday night. I gotta work." Aceman grinned proudly, relishing the few chuckles his joke received.

"I don't even know how to begin to respond to that offensively *in*correct response," Mr. Wise said. "Mr. Dooley, would you care to end this charade?"

"He and I will be there Saturday night," Jon answered in his flat voice.

Mr. Wise made a deep bow in his direction. "Thank you, kind sir, for releasing us from this endless round of misery!" He turned and wrote the correct sentence on the board.

I didn't pay much attention to the snickers around the room because something else was bothering me. Mr. Wise had never been in our school before, as far as I knew, and yet he had called on everyone by name. Maybe Mrs. Markle had left a seating chart for him, but I hadn't seen him check any papers.

Albert raised his hand and Mr. Wise called on him by name, too.

"How are we supposed to know what's right?"

"Because there are rules," the teacher replied. "Simple rules. *Grammar rules*." He wrote those last two words on the board. "'He' and 'I' both serve as the subject of the sentence. You wouldn't say 'me is going' anymore than you would say 'him is going.' The same applies when you put them together as a subject."

He wrote another sentence on the board: "'It's a special day for Mary and I.' What do you think about this one?" he asked.

Jon's hand shot up but Mr. Wise ignored it. Instead, he carefully looked over the room, searching for his next victim. "Mr. Perini?"

You couldn't hear a gasp, but you could sense one. All the teachers knew better than to call on Sam Perini, because he has a speech problem that embarrasses him and the rest of the class, as well. "Mr. Perini, can you correct this sentence?"

Sam shook his head. He wouldn't have, even if he knew the answer. "I can't hear you," Mr. Wise said. I held my breath waiting for Sam to start tripping over his own tongue. Miraculously, Sam opened his mouth and spoke perfectly, without a glitch. Even he seemed surprised. "It's a special day for I and Mary?" he asked.

"*Incorrect*," said Mr. Wise, more gently than before. He circled "Mary and" on the board. "Would you say, 'It's a special day for I'? Would you, Mr. Perini?"

"Would me? I mean, would I?" Sam gulped.

When it was clear that Sam was out of guesses, the teacher turned to the princess. "How about you, Miss Eglantine Peabody? Surely a person of your stature should know proper grammar."

Thankfully, I was the only person in class who seemed to notice the "of your stature" bit and my muscles tensed. Eglantine, however, was unruffled. "It is a special day for Mary and *me*," she answered.

"Perfect," said Mr. Wise with a self-satisfied grin.

"Precisely what I expected." As he bowed, I got a creepy feeling.

"Both 'Mary' and 'me' act as the object of the preposition 'for.' It would be as incorrect to say 'for Mary and I' as it would be to say 'for I.' Rules, people. Rules." The substitute pointed to the words he'd written on the board. "Grammar rules. Grammar *rules*! Say it, people. *Grammar rules*!"

Usually kids pretty much ignore what a substitute says, but this time was an exception as everyone began to chant. "Grammar rules! Grammar rules!" They even stomped their feet, the way the crowd had cheered at Egg's cheerleading tryout.

Mr. Wise shouted over the noise, "If you learn the rules contained in this magical book"—he thumped his grammar book—"you will have the keys to the kingdom! You will be on the royal road to fame and fortune! Because why, people? GRAMMAR RULES!"

There was more chanting and stomping and then the bell rang. As my classmates filed out, they were a lot more excited about grammar than I'd ever seen them. But I was kind of shaken. Especially when Mr. Wise singled me out and said, "I am sorry I did not have an opportunity to call on you, Miss Casey Peabody."

I rushed out of the room.

I'd just about recovered from my shakiness when I opened my locker and Ric stepped out. Yep, right out of my locker. "You really shouldn't do stuff like that," I told him, shaking all over again. "Somebody will see you."

"Only if I let them," he reminded me. "So how'd you like Mr. Wise?"

"There's something weird about him."

"What's weird is that he's not a substitute *or* Mr. Wise. Casey, *that* was Boricius."

I was astounded. "You mean your teacher?"

"More than a mere teacher. A grand master."

I was stunned. "Why did you bring him here?"

"I didn't. It was all his idea. I tried to stop him but when Boricius makes up his mind . . ." Ric shook his head. "He's figured out the spell and he wants to take the princess back to Trewellyn."

I was speechless.

"Now," Ric added. "I thought he'd do it in class, but I think he got caught up in teaching. Man, he loves attention."

"Why does he have to do it now?"

"He can't wait to show off his superior skills." Ric's green eyes were cloudy with worry. "He's a grandstander . . . a showoff."

"You've got to stop him!"

"What can I do? He's my teacher—a grand master! He outranks me, and to tell the truth, I think he withholds some of the big stuff from me. Which, by the way, is a major no-no for a teacher."

I gritted my teeth. "You *have* to try."

"Casey, Boricius is much more powerful than I am. It's something I have to accept."

I could hear Egg's voice in my head, talking about homecoming. "But she's looking forward to home-coming. And she'd want to say good-bye to Tino. Why does he have to do it so fast?"

"Because he can."

"So you think, like, she'll just be in the hall and he'll make her disappear?"

"Nope. Knowing Boricius, he'll wait till he has a big audience. A big class, a game, maybe. The more eyes on him, the better."

The situation sounded grim. I checked my watch. "Got to go. Bell's going to ring." I was about to rush off.

"Actually it won't ring until you get to class. You can count on that." Ric flashed me one of his famous grins. At least I could count on Ric for something.

I didn't hurry to get to class, knowing that Ric would make sure the bell didn't ring until I got there. I felt sorry for him because Boricius had shown up and taken over. I felt sorry for Egg, too. She might vanish into thin air before everyone's eyes—what could be more embarrassing than that? And I most definitely felt sorry for myself, especially when I realized that if the princess left, Ric would leave, too. Forever.

"You look like you just lost your best friend," Alisha whispered as I slid into my seat. If I smiled back at her, I didn't mean it.

Egg was already sitting in the cafeteria with Tino when I arrived at lunchtime. They invited me to join them, but since I figured they might not have too much time left together, I said no. I grabbed a salad and a bottle of water and looked for a soccer team-mate to sit with. Instead, I heard Ric calling me. He wasn't alone, either. He was with a guy—okay, a *cute* guy—who looked kind of familiar.

Did I mention he was cute?

Ric introduced him as Colin Browning. Square jaw, crooked smile, dark brown eyes, black spiky hair. I didn't know him, but I knew he was on the track team.

"I know you," he said. "Soccer player, right?" He wasn't necessarily psychic. It was a game day and I was wearing my team jersey.

I suddenly remembered my fading black eye and tried to pull my hair over it.

"I hope that's a sports-related shiner," he said, still smiling.

I nodded.

"Cool," he said. "I gave myself a black eye one time. I was catching a pop fly. I bobbled it and it popped right up in my eye. Took me a while to live that one down."

"You run track—right?" I asked.

"Pole vault, actually."

"Impressive," I added.

"So what do you do besides soccer?"

"Me? Play softball. Shortstop."

Colin smiled. "Shortstop. So you're not exactly afraid of being put on the spot?"

"Oh . . . and you *are*, Mr. Pole-Vaulter? Not exactly an event for someone who wants to play it safe."

He grinned. "I did consider the high dive."

"Me too," I admitted. "But I never had the nerve to take the plunge."

That made us both laugh and I relaxed a little. I tried not to listen to the little voice in my head that said, "You're talking to a *boy!*" Somehow we talked about everything from softball to track to the Olympics. Ric didn't say much but his head turned from side to side as if he were watching a tennis match.

I guess Colin realized Ric was left out, so he asked him what kind of sports he liked. "I like the occasional sword fight."

"Fencing—now that's a cool sport," Colin said.

"But there's more to life than sports, guys," Ric suggested.

I was about to say, "There is?" Luckily Colin spoke first. "I figured that out last year. I'm into playing the guitar now, and my friends and I started a band." He flashed me another crooked grin. "What do you do besides play sports, Casey?"

I was stumped, but I didn't want to sound dull.

"Well, sports are definitely my main thing. And my grandmother and I go to yard sales and buy things that she resells sometimes."

"Oh, an entrepreneur?" Colin gulped down the last of his OJ. "I like that."

"Casey, aren't you interested in medieval things?" Ric was pushing it. "Spells and castles and stuff?"

"A little."

I flashed Ric a warning look to drop it but Colin seemed to think medieval stuff was cool, thank goodness. Then he got into his interest in alternative music and some cutting-edge Finnish band he'd been listening to. I told him that I came across weird CDs sometimes at yard sales, so I'd let him know if I found anything cool.

I was in a daze, I think, because there was a very cool guy talking to me and I didn't have to squeal or squeak like a chipmunk or pretend to be somebody I wasn't. And when Ric mentioned I had a soccer game that day, Colin said he might check it out. (Okay, I guess I squealed a little on the inside.)

The great thing was that time passed really slowly, as if we were talking for an hour. It was probably a trick of Ric's, and I should have been irritated at him for meddling in my life with magic.

But I wasn't.

18.

Ye Most Strange Turn of Events

"**Remember**, the game isn't all about you. You're playing for the team today," Coach Curson told us in the locker room before the game. The pressure was definitely on.

Coach says if the adrenaline isn't flowing, you can't give a peak performance. I was suffering from a combination of adrenaline, butterflies, and princess worries because (A) Egg insisted on cheering at my game, and (B) thanks to Boricius, she could disappear before everyone's eyes. David Beckham never had such worries!

When I got on the field, first I checked out our opponents, the Harvey Red Hawks. Then I checked out the stands. There was a small crowd. Gran, Shane, and Dad were all there—no surprise. There was no Ric in sight, though that didn't necessarily mean he wasn't present. I hoped he was working on a plan to help the princess avoid Boricius, but I knew that for Alaric, challenging Boricius would be like me defying Coach.

There was another familiar face in the crowd, too: Colin. I like people who keep their promises, even if they give me butterflies in my stomach.

The whistle blew and I launched into game mode. The Red Hawks got control of the ball early, catching us off guard with their aggressive play. Where was our defense? Maybe they were as distracted as I was by the unfamiliar sounds of spectators chanting, "Hey, get that ball! Hey, get that ball!"

A fleeting glance told me all I needed to know. Standing in front of the stands in full cheerleader regalia was Princess Eglantine of Trewellyn, leading the cheers all by herself:

> Go-Panthers-go!
> Go-Panthers-go!

I looked back to the field and was shocked to see the Red Hawks' striker bearing down on the goal. There was Carly, our poor excuse for a goalkeeper, obviously not sure which direction to turn. I was thinking, "Well, it's just one goal," when an amazing thing happened. Carly flew through the air—practically airborne—and stopped the ball!

"Car-ly! Car-ly! Car-ly!" Egg and the crowd chanted.

It was such an unbelievable play, it was almost like magic—which made me suspicious. I checked out the stands again to see if Ric had appeared. Instead, I saw someone large and bulky moving along the sidelines.

The ball was in play, but I kept watching because the large person turned out to be Mr. Wise—Boricius, that is—and he was marching toward the stands, right toward Egg. The long streamers in her hair were flying as she jumped and cheered:

Move that ball, go,
Move that ball, go . . .

I was so sure Boricius was about to make Egg vanish in front of everyone, I saw the future flash through my mind: Gran and Shane feeling disappointed and sad. Dad relieved but angry. The rest of the crowd shocked, and Tino's heart completely broken. I could almost hear him saying, "She never even said good-bye."

Worse yet, Egg would never know what hit her. One minute, she'd be cheering in Pine Glen. The next minute, she'd be sitting on a throne holding her pompoms. She'd probably feel naked without her tiara. And who would be there to greet her except a smelly duke and a sickly fiancé?

Boricius paused a few feet away from the princess, his eyes fixed on her. Slowly he raised his arms. I was positive the grand master had something up his sleeve, like a one-way ticket back to Trewellyn for the princess. I hoped with all my heart that Ric would stop him, but there wasn't much time left.

"Heads up, Peabody," the coach shouted.

I looked back on the field as Heather passed the ball to me, coming fast in a straight line. It would be a simple move to stop it and kick a header straight into the net, giving us our first—and possibly winning—goal.

I quickly checked the sidelines again. Boricius stood behind the princess, raising his arms. Was that a ruler in his hand—or a wand? Without a second thought, I stopped the ball and kicked it hard—but not toward the goal. I kicked that baby straight toward Boricius.

It traveled hard and fast, smacking the old man squarely against the side of his sizable head. Whistles blew and the crowd let out a shared gasp.

He fell to the ground about as hard as Tino had fallen for the princess.

The game stopped while all attention focused on Boricius's crumpled figure. A bunch of people rushed to his side, including Dad. Egg was frozen as she stared first at the fallen teacher, then at me. I saw Boricius move his arms—thank goodness I hadn't killed him. I'd only meant to slow him down. Suddenly I saw Ric right in the thick of things. I guess he'd been watching all along.

My teammates and I remained motionless on the field. Within a few minutes, an ambulance pulled up. In short order, Boricius was placed on a stretcher, carried into the ambulance with Ric at his side, and driven away.

The motionless players stirred back to life when the whistle blew to restart play. "On the bench," Coach Curson growled at me, "for the rest of the game. We'll talk about this later."

I knew better than to argue with Coach, so I took my place of disgrace on the sidelines. It was like a giant time-out; I might as well have been wearing a dunce cap. I weighed the consequences of what I'd done. My teammates were no doubt steamed at me. Gran and Dad were most likely embarrassed. And Ric was probably mad at me for beaning his grand master. I figured the old wizard could cast a spell to undo whatever I'd done to him. My biggest worry was that Colin thought I was a total idiot and a really terrible soccer player!

Facing all that humiliation, I barely noticed when the Red Hawks scored a goal. If we lost, I'd really face Coach's wrath. All this to help out the princess, who might not even appreciate what I'd done. For all I knew, she wished she was home in her father's dank castle with fish-faced Prince Bore-land.

I was so deep in thought, it took me awhile to notice the crowd was cheering in that "go team go" way. I looked over and saw Egg bouncing up and down in front. But what were they saying?

Give her another chance.
Ca-sey! Ca-sey!
Give her another chance.
Ca-sey! Ca-sey!

While I'd been feeling sorry for myself, the princess was doing her best to get me back into the game, which made me feel even worse!

Coach Curson was chatting away on her cell phone. A few seconds later, she approached the bench. "Peabody, I have good news for you. The man you hit with the ball isn't seriously injured. I think he was mostly dazed."

Too dazed to cast a spell on the princess, just as I planned.

"Maybe I was too rough on you. I mean, it's not like you intentionally kicked the ball at him, right?"

I kept quiet on that one.

"Why don't you go back in and try to redeem yourself?" Coach suggested.

She didn't have to ask me twice! I was on the field in a flash. Carly continued to stop our opponents' goal attempts. That made the Red Hawks even more aggressive and I got fouled.

Taking a penalty kick is a nerve-wracking experience, mainly because everybody expects you to make it. Hearing the crowd cheering, "Make that point, *hey*! Make that point!" didn't make me any calmer. Still, I nailed it and scored.

I guess we couldn't expect our formerly klutzy Carly to be perfect. In the second half, the Red Hawks answered back by slotting a ball into the back of the net. The game was tied. Time was running out and the crowd grew boisterous, thanks to the princess's spirited leadership. Those jousting knights were really missing out on a good thing.

It was late in the game when Lindsey passed the ball to me and I was in position to score the winning point. I'm pretty sure I could have, but I spotted Alisha a little closer to the goal. I took a deep breath and passed it to her. She quickly volleyed it into the net and the Red Hawks' keeper didn't know what hit her.

Alisha scored the winning point . . . and I scored some points with Coach, who gave me a big thumbs-up. Her congratulatory speech afterward was all about working together as a team. Carly was named Player of the Day, and she deserved it. But I got something better when Coach took me aside and whispered, "*Now* you're the player I hoped you'd be."

"Good job," I told Carly on my way out of the locker room.

"Thanks!" she said, beaming. "I've really been practicing hard lately." I guess practice is a kind of magic, too.

Gran, Dad, and Shane were waiting outside for me. First I got a good Gran-hug. "I felt terrible for you when that poor man got hit!" she told me.

"It didn't rattle this girl," Dad said proudly. "Beautiful penalty kick and perfect pass! *And* I hear that poor old guy's doing well."

"That was not some poor old guy," I told them. "*That* was Boricius."

I didn't get to tell them everything, because I noticed Colin standing nearby. Gran quickly sized up the situation and shuttled Dad and Shane out to the car to wait for me. That left Colin and me standing face-to-face.

"Great game," he said. "I was impressed with the way you came back after the, you know, accident."

"I don't know what happened there." Okay,

I stretched the truth.

"Could happen to anyone. He was in the wrong place at the wrong time."

Yeah. The wrong place in the wrong century.

"Anyway," he continued, "maybe you can fill me in on the finer points of soccer sometime. I'm catching on, but I have some questions."

I swallowed hard. "Sure. Anytime."

We stood there grinning at each other for a while until he said, "I guess your family's waiting for you."

"Oops. Yeah, you're right. I should be going." I could have stood there forever but instead I thanked him for coming to my game and raced toward the parking lot.

"What on earth makes you think that substitute teacher is Boricius?" Gran asked later that evening.

"Ric told me."

We were all eating dinner after the game. We used to get subs after the games, but Gran was on a health kick, so she'd made a pot of vegetable soup instead.

"I thought he seemed . . . familiar," Egg said. "It was strange the way he looked at me in class."

"No way!" Shane said. "Boricius is a grand master wizard! Now I'll never get to meet him. You probably killed him."

Gran quickly explained that Ric had called from the emergency room to say that Boricius was fine.

"Okay, say he was Boricius," Dad said. "Why did you deliberately kick the ball at him? Because I know you, Casey. That kick was deliberate."

I stirred my soup with my spoon a few times. "Ric told me that Boricius knew the spell to get Egg back to Trewellyn and he was going to use it right away."

The princess gasped. "Back home!"

"It would be wrong of him to make her disappear in front of a whole crowd. Plus she wouldn't get to cheer for homecoming or go to the dance or say good-bye to Tino. Or us. I mean, I think Egg should choose when she wants to go back."

I turned toward the princess, hoping she'd agree. She was staring down at her soup.

"I know not what to say."

"I have something to say," Shane interjected. "I would give *anything* to meet Boricius! Now he's probably mad at you and I never will. He'll probably put an evil spell on the whole family! Did you think of that?"

"Hush, Shane," Gran said. "Let's not talk like that."

"I don't get it," Dad muttered. "I thought Boricius was going to give the spell to Alaric so he could handle it himself."

I explained about how Boricius had decided not

to share the information and how helpless Ric felt about the situation.

Egg finally stopped staring at her soup and stared at me instead. "Are you saying you kicked the ball at Boricius . . . to help me stay here? With you?"

"I guess." I had to admit it.

Egg's eyes filled with tears. I hate tears.

"Besides, if you'd disappeared into thin air, it would have caused a commotion and ruined the game," I quickly explained.

Just then, Ric strolled in with a big smile on his face.

"Sorry to barge in unannounced," he said.

"Don't you always?" Dad replied.

Ric pulled up a chair and made himself at home. "I thought you'd like to know that everything worked out with, uh . . . you did tell them, didn't you, Casey?"

I nodded.

"With Boricius," he finished.

"Is he going to put an evil spell on Casey?" Shane asked.

Ric chuckled. "No, no, that's not proper wizard behavior. You don't put an evil spell on somebody for spite. Besides, he doesn't know much about soccer. I've managed to convince him it was an unfortunate accident."

"Is the poor man still in the hospital?" Gran asked, ladling out a bowl of soup for Ric.

"No. There was a huge scene at the hospital because he didn't have health insurance or any proper identification. Seems Boricius wasn't as prepared as he might have been. Anyway, he got so frustrated at the questions and the paperwork, he made himself invisible and split."

"You mean he disappeared?"

"Well, you never know when he'll be back. I mean, he *is* Boricius. But I think I've managed to talk him into teaching me the right spell."

"What changed his mind?" I asked.

Ric grinned. "I think he just needed a good knock on the head."

Everyone chuckled except Egg, who gave out a heartrending sob.

"Oh, woe is me! Woe, woe . . ." I didn't hear the rest of her outburst because she pushed back her chair and raced to the bedroom, slamming the door behind her. Duke crawled under my chair, whining.

We all turned to Ric, who looked a bit sheepish. "I guess somebody should have asked the princess how she felt about the whole thing."

We sat in uncomfortable silence except for a random whimper from Duke. Then I finally got up, too. "Come on, Duke," I said. "I think you can help out here."

19.

Ye Changes and Challenges

The princess was drying her tears when Duke and I barged in. I plopped down on my bed and Duke jumped up on Egg's.

"I think I owe you an apology. Big-time," I told her. "I took away your one sure chance to go home without asking you first. And I didn't even bother to thank you for cheering for me and getting me back in the game."

She managed a bit of a smile and blew her nose. I didn't know princesses ever did that.

"Anyway," I continued, "I hope you can forgive me."

Egg held her chin high. "Of course. I can get people thrown into the dungeon, but I can also have them pardoned."

A pardon wasn't exactly what I wanted, but I didn't argue.

The princess suddenly flung herself down on her bed, her head next to Duke's.

"Casey, I know not what to do! I want to stay here for homecoming and go to the dance with Tino. Still, now that Boricius has the spell, there is no reason not to return home. My duty is to my father. He has no other heirs—he needs me! Would you not want to help your father if he were in need?"

I tried to imagine being separated from my father by more than a few centuries, like Egg was. "I guess you have to follow your heart."

Egg sat up straight. "Father says that is what the commoners do. But as royalty, we must put our duties before our hearts."

My own heart was feeling pretty heavy about the princess's situation. I guess Duke's was, too. He began to lick her face.

"Oh, Duke, you always did tend to drool." She scratched his head. "Still, I'm quite fond of you. If I decide to go back, you must go back with me."

My sympathy for Egg faded. "Duke was our dog for three years before you ever got here. He's not *your* duke. He's *our* Duke. And he's staying here."

The princess sat up, her lower lip trembling. "But . . . he must. He's my friend."

Her eyes welled up with tears again. I certainly hadn't made her feel any better.

"Sorry to interrupt, Princess." Gran stuck her head in the door. "Mrs. Temple is on the phone."

Mrs. Temple was faculty advisor to the cheerleading squad and what she told Egg made her feel even worse. It turns out there's a code that says cheerleaders are strictly forbidden to go off on their own to cheer for whomever they want. They're only allowed to cheer at authorized games for authorized guys. They can't even wear their uniforms without permission. So the princess was now on probation. She could still cheer with the rest of the cheerleaders, but if she broke one more rule she'd be off the squad for good.

"Does this mean I cannot cheer for your soccer team?" she asked when she hung up the phone.

"Not officially. Not in your cheerleading clothes."

"But I *can* cheer for you."

"Well . . . yes. But I don't want you to risk getting kicked off the squad. Besides, you're fighting a losing battle.

You'd have thought I said her tiara was fake. "There is no such thing as a losing battle! My father, the king, taught me that! A will begets a way!"

With that, Egg stormed out, leaving me alone, feeling the full power of a princess's fury.

Egg was quiet the rest of the week. When she wasn't at cheerleading practice, she was scribbling in a notebook. I was edgy, thinking I saw Boricius around every corner, and the rest of my thoughts were taken up with Colin. I was careful not to get too carried away with the idea of anything approaching an actual boyfriend, but we had lunch together almost every day and he kept showing up at my locker. He even asked me if I'd sit with him at the football game on Saturday and go to the Pizza Palace afterward. That was a no-brainer. I said yes.

On Saturday morning, Gran announced she was going to a yard sale—the first since the princess incident—and she invited me to go along. I wasn't exactly enthusiastic, since our last find was a disaster of major proportions, but on the other hand, I was afraid to let Gran go by herself. Who knew what she might pick up on her own? Dad tried to talk her out of going, too, but she insisted we Peabodys should get back to normal. Since Egg's arrival we'd been anything *but*.

So while the princess went off to cheerleading practice in preparation for the game, Gran, Duke, and I set off in search of undiscovered treasures.

Instead of the creepy old mansion, this time we

stopped at a suburban ranch house. The driveway was overflowing with toys and play equipment, a crib and a bassinet. There were plenty of people pricing bikes and board games, but Gran decided to check out a pile of linens and sent me over to a puny rack of clothes near the garage door. As soon as I got there, a flash of orange caught my eye. Not a bright orange, more like a burnt orange. A fitted, zip-up sweater with a collar. On a whim, I put it on, and like a flash, Gran was right at my side.

"Casey, that sweater looks great on you! Take it," Gran urged.

The lady who owned the house came galloping up. "Isn't that adorable on her? That'll be three dollars."

Before I had a chance to say anything, Gran peeled off three bucks and steered me back to the car.

"I'm not sure . . . ," I argued, even though it was obviously a done deal.

"What do you say we stop at the mall? I need some shoes," Gran said as she practically pushed me into her station wagon.

Duke whimpered. I guess he realized we weren't going to stop for muffins.

I knew the mall was part of Gran's grand plan to make me more fashionable, but for once I didn't feel like fighting it. It wasn't until I got home that I realized Gran hadn't looked for a pair of shoes for herself after all. But I loved the pair she'd bought me.

A while later, the whole family left to go to the game and watch Egg cheer. When we reached the stands, I summoned up the nerve to say, "I said I'd sit with a friend . . . if that's okay with you." Dad raised his eyebrows, but Gran quickly said, "Sure, that's not a problem."

I hurried toward the fifty-yard line, where Colin was waiting for me.

"You look great," he said.

I hoped my blushing face didn't clash with my new orange sweater.

Colin was fun to be with. We analyzed the game together, and he had a lot of friends who came over to say hi and joke around. Ric was nowhere in sight, and after a while, I forgot to look for him.

I could hardly forget about the princess, though. She gave the cheerleading squad a commanding presence and the crowd seemed to have more fun with her around. Of course, our team also happened to win!

The scene at the Pizza Palace afterward was like a dream. A weird dream, but a good one. Tino taught Colin to say "chilly" instead of "cool" and Colin tried to explain pole-vaulting to Egg, who feared it was like impaling yourself on your sword.

When it was time to leave, Colin nervously ran his fingers through his hair and said, "This is kind of embarrassing, but I have something to ask you. I didn't ask anybody to homecoming because there wasn't anybody I wanted to go with. Then I met you. I know it's late to be asking, but is there any chance you could go with me? I mean, I'm not really a dance person but I thought it would be fun to hang out with you. I mean, if you'd like to." He rolled his eyes. "I don't think that even made sense."

I know those lists of rules for girls always say not to accept invitations at the last minute. But luckily, as much as I like soccer and softball, I don't play those *other* kinds of girl games. I said yes without hesitation.

Gran was pleased with my news. "Great! So what are you going to wear?"

There's always a catch, isn't there? We had less than a week to wrangle over that question. Even I knew jeans were out. And my fall-back black-skirt-white-shirt combo wasn't going to cut it either.

Alisha, who was going to the dance with Taj, gave me the rundown on what to wear: The homecoming court (a queen and four princesses) wore formal clothes. Everybody else wore something semiformal, whatever that meant.

On Monday, there was a special announcement over the school intercom. The election for homecoming court had been held the first week of school, but the votes had just been tallied. It turned out that Rachel Hanrahan had been elected princess—but since the poor girl had been unexpectedly whisked off to Switzerland, an emergency election had been held that morning. Guess who won?

"Well, 'tis only fitting that I be a princess" was Egg's response to her victory. "Perhaps even queen."

"Sorry, Egg. There's no way that crown is going to anyone but Eden. Only a ninth-grader can be the queen. That's the rule."

The princess kept her chin high. "Don't worry. I shall be queen some day."

I'm not sure if she meant queen of Trewellyn or Pine Glen Junior High—probably both.

20.

Ye Surprising Plan

On the day when the weekly *Pine Glen Gazette* comes out, most of the issues end up on the floor. Once you've flipped through to see if your name is mentioned anywhere, the *Gazette* gets boring fast. So I was surprised to see so many kids walking around actually reading the paper that Tuesday.

"What's so interesting?" I asked Egg on the way to lunch.

"I have not the foggiest notion."

As we sat down with Tino and Colin, the guys straightened me out.

"Yo—Egg, that letter is chilly," Tino said.

"Funny, I never thought about it before but you're

right," Colin agreed.

I quickly thumbed through the pages and there it was, on the editorial page, a pretty long letter to the editor in a box with the headline:

ARE PINE GLEN GIRL ATHLETES
GETTING THE ROYAL SHAFT?
by Eglantine Peabody

The first few sentences had me really nervous.

Once upon a time, a fair-haired princess was magically transported to the land of Pine Glen. At first, the princess was frightened because the people she encountered were friendly, but looked and acted differently from the populace of the kingdom she had come from.

"Oh, no," I murmured. Egg was blowing her cover . . . in print! I read on.

Surprisingly, even though the princess dressed and spoke differently than the citizens of the new land, they accepted her. Before long, she realized that Pine Glen was a wondrous place where everyone was treated equally: all races, all religions, men and women.

"Oh, joy," thought the princess. "Pine Glen. 'Tis the perfect land where one may live happily ever after!"

And happy she was, until she learned that Pine Glen had a deep, dark secret: For all their talk, men and women were not treated equally after all. For when the men played their games of sport, large crowds gathered to watch and groups of women dressed up in costumes to cheer them on. But alas—when the women played their games of sport, few people came to watch and women were strictly forbidden to dress in costumes and cheer them on.

The princess spoke to the citizens of Pine Glen, but they wouldn't listen. Until one day, she came forward and said very loudly, "Go cheer for the girls—I command you!"

A hushed silence followed, because people in Pine Glen didn't command one another to do things. So the princess apologized. Instead she said, *"GO CHEER FOR THE GIRLS AGAINST HILLSIDE HIGH THIS FRIDAY—I BESEECH YOU! AND YOU WILL HAVE A GOOD TIME, FOR THOSE FAIR LADIES ARE AWESOME PLAYERS!"*

The citizens of Pine Glen went to the game and lo—they were royally entertained. And they all—men and women alike—lived happily ever after!

"Egg, it's just *great*!" I stammered.

Tino beamed as proudly as if he'd written it himself. "How'd you come up with that princess thing? That was brilliant."

"I was inspired," Egg said with a catlike smile.

Colin shook his head. "It is kind of strange, isn't it? I mean, that nobody's ever cheered for the girls before."

"Yeah, but maybe things will change," I said. "Like when they finally let women vote."

"Women weren't allowed to vote?" I thought the princess was going to fall off her chair but Tino gladly steadied her.

"That was a long time ago," he told her.

I guess he was her biggest admirer, though he certainly wasn't the only one. Not by a long shot.

The main point of homecoming was the football game against Hillside on Saturday, followed by the dance, but Egg's letter to the editor let people know that our girls' soccer game against Hillside was on Friday afternoon. It was nice to get some press, at least.

Hillside was a big game for us, but I have to admit it wasn't the only thing on my mind. Coach Curson said I was playing better than ever, but it was much harder to "get in the groove" as far as the dance went. It would have been nice if Ric had zapped his magic wand to provide me with the perfect outfit, but Ric wasn't around to be my fairy godmother, so Gran did her best by suggesting one outfit after another.

Then one night, Egg said, "Gran, don't you think Casey should decide what's right for her to wear?"

"I could use some help," I admitted. "I mean, I don't want to wear something really frilly. But I don't want to be embarrassed, either."

"Pish! If you are wearing what you truly want to wear, there is no reason to be embarrassed. The only reason to be embarrassed is if you're wearing something you do not like."

"Doesn't it embarrass you the way all the girls at school are imitating you?"

"*Trying* to imitate me," she insisted. "It does not bother me, but it should bother them."

"Your old pal Maddy's started wearing ribbons around her legs," I said. "I guess she figures if you can't lick 'em, join 'em. Problem is, they make her calves look fat."

"That's what Tino said," the princess noted on her way out the door.

The phone rang and I ran to get it. *Okay,* I thought, *it might be Colin.* But as soon as I picked it up, familiar purple smoke came pouring out the little holes in the receiver.

"Where *are* you?" I asked.

"Boricius has been showing me the nuances of the spell," Ric answered. "Sorry I haven't been around."

"Did you help Egg write that editorial for the paper?"

"What editorial?" Ric didn't sound like he was kidding.

"Never mind. You were saying . . ."

"I know it's late, but well, if it's not *too* late, I'd like to ask you to go to the homecoming dance with me."

Whoa—my mind was instantly in a muddle! Two weeks ago, I would have been thrilled, but times had changed.

"Well, I'd like to . . . but I'm already going with Colin."

It was Ric's turn to be muddled, but he quickly recovered. "Colin? Good guy. That's great."

"I thought you arranged the whole thing in the first place."

"Who, me?"

"Didn't you put a spell on him so he'd like me or something?" I asked.

Ric laughed. "That's not what happened. Colin said he'd seen you hanging out with me, and he asked if I'd introduce him. That's not a spell. It's . . . chemistry. Casey, he likes you because of *you*, not because of anything I did."

I wish I could have seen those green eyes, so I'd know for sure that Ric was being truthful. But part of me was starting to believe I could do okay without the help of magic. For the first time in my life, two really nice guys had asked me to the same dance.

When I hung up the phone, I felt as if I'd just gotten off a roller coaster. I guess that's why they call some girls "boy crazy." Boys can really make you crazy, all right.

By the end of the week, nobody at school was concentrating much on schoolwork, except maybe the princess. In French class, M. asked her, "*Est-ce que vous allez au bal de la rentrée, mademoiselle?*"

Without hesitation, Egg serenely responded in her perfect French accent, "*Oui, monsieur. Je serai une princesse.*" Monsieur didn't know how true that statement was.

Me—I was a bundle of nerves. Coach had already warned us about Hillside's strong defense. But if I wasn't worrying about the game, I was worrying about the dance—what to wear, how to act, what to say, how to move! Alisha gave me a crash course, but I was afraid my feet were too used to playing sports to learn how to dance.

That Friday afternoon, I had to keep reminding myself to focus on the game. When we took the field, a huge cheer went up:

> *Panther girls rule!*
> *Panther girls rule!*
> *Go Panthers! Go girls!*
> *Go-go-go!*

A quick peek at the stands revealed an amazing sight. Seated in the first three rows was a large group of guys wearing Panther shirts and waving pennants. Colin was there, along with Noah, Albert, Aceman, and a bunch more. Leading them in the cheering was none other than Ric.

Egg sat farther up in the stands with Gran, Dad, and Shane. They had pennants and were cheering loudly, too. I was relieved to see that Egg was *not* wearing her cheerleading uniform.

The whistle blew, the ball was in play, and I went

into full game mode. We squeaked by, winning 5–4. I scored two of those points, but the big news was that formerly feeble Heather scored a goal for the first time ever . . . on a pass from *moi*!

"Are you asleep?" I asked Egg late that night.

She yawned loudly (for a princess) and said, "No."

"I wanted to tell you something. I think you should run for student government next year. You're really a great leader."

Egg turned on the light. "Thank you. I've been trained to be a leader since birth. That's what princesses do."

"But look at all you've accomplished without anyone knowing you're a princess!"

Next, Egg did something quite surprising: She moved over to my bed and sat next to me. "Casey," she said. "I will not be running for student government next year."

Her tone of voice worried me.

"Too busy?" I asked.

"All this talk about homecoming has made me realize 'tis time for me to go home. Alaric got the spell from Boricius and I can leave at any time."

I felt a cold shiver run down my spine. "Are you really sure?"

"If something should happen to Father, who would lead Trewellyn? 'Tis my duty."

"When?"

"Tomorrow night after homecoming. I'll say farewell to Tino then."

"Do you really want to go?" I asked her warily.

"I have two families now and 'tis hard to choose between them," she said. "Still, 'tis lonely in that tower."

"Like the Lady of Shalott," I murmured.

"My life in Trewellyn was like looking in a mirror, but here, I have truly lived." A few tears dropped from Egg's sky-blue eyes. Then a very magical thing happened. Princess Eglantine Eleanor Annalisa Ambrosia de Bercy gave me a royally sweet hug. And I hugged her right back.

21.

Ye Homecoming and
Ye Home-Going

Everything about homecoming had a strange happy-sad air about it. It was the best weekend ever. But it was also the last weekend ever for the princess and the Peabodys.

Egg outdid herself cheering for the Panther football team as they trounced Hillside Saturday afternoon. Afterward, everybody rushed home to get ready for the dance. It was hard to believe that three hours after cheering our lungs out in the hot Indian summer sun, we were all showering and primping to become our most sophisticated selves.

At seven, Egg emerged from the bedroom wearing the gown she had arrived in—freshly pressed by Gran—and her tiara, freshly polished. We talked her out of wearing the tiara because only the homecoming queen is supposed to wear a crown. So instead, she wore a simple circle of daisies in her hair. I followed her in my getup, which turned out to be my old standby black skirt, a sleeveless black lace top that Alisha loaned me, and a really *chilly* ice-blue satin jacket from the fifties that I found in Gran's closet.

Dad wolf-whistled when he saw us—how embarrassing was that! "Look who stepped off the cover of *Vogue*!" he said. As he hugged me, he whispered that I reminded him of Mom. "And for a girl who doesn't know how to talk to boys," he added, "you're doing pretty well."

Then he took *lots* of pictures. An album full.

Tino arrived in a tux, looking like the kind of Prince Charming that every princess deserves. Mr. Abruzzo was driving and they had already picked up Colin. When Colin walked in holding a corsage for me, my heart did a major flip. He was wearing a black suit jacket over one of his favorite T-shirts, with these really cool black jeans. He might not have been a match for a princess, but he looked just right to me.

Alisha was having a get-together after the dance and Colin's mom was going to drive us home from there. Dad said he wanted us back home by 11:30 *on the dot,* and I wanted to talk him into another half hour, but the princess quickly agreed. "Yes, I must be back here before midnight, like Cinderella," she said. "Please, will you all wait up for us?" When a princess has a plan, it's best not to interfere.

Miraculously Colin and I managed to move around the dance floor without me kicking him like a soccer ball or him pole-vaulting over my head! In fact, looking around, we were positively graceful compared with Albert Falutti pushing Maddy around the floor. Rumor has it that *she* asked *him* out of sheer desperation. I guess she forgot to ask him if he knew how to dance first. She kept a fake smile frozen on her face as Albert shuffled her aimlessly around the floor. On the other hand, Egg danced like a contestant in one of those ballroom dancing shows on TV.

My feet were more used to sneakers than dancing shoes, and I got a little wobbly after a while, so Colin suggested we sit down. When he intertwined his fingers with mine, I felt a kind of magic that I knew didn't have anything to do with wizards or spells. We talked about Finnish rock, Irish rugby, and Italian food. He was so easy to be with. I knew I'd remember this dance for a long time.

Then, it was time to crown the homecoming queen. People stopped dancing and moved to the sidelines of the gym so that the royal court of Pine

Glen could proceed up to the stage. I was pretty relaxed, knowing the princess would out-royal the rest until I saw something very disturbing. In fact, I gasped.

"What is it?" Colin asked.

I couldn't tell him that I'd seen Mr. Wise mingling with the other teachers who were chaperoning the dance. Mr. Wise—Boricius—had promised Ric that he'd let *him* take the princess back to Trewellyn, but it looked as if his plans had changed.

"Casey, are you okay?" Colin asked. His dark brown eyes showed true concern, but as happy as I was to be his date, I suddenly wished that Ric was there with me. I wasn't sure where he was—probably in some netherworld between Pine Glen and Trewellyn, practicing the spell.

"I have a bad feeling about something," I told Colin.

"Probably the punch. Why does it always have to be green?"

I knew why *I* was turning green. There was only one reason for Boricius to be at the dance: to one-up Alaric, to prove he was a superior wizard, and to show off in public for the first time in a bunch of centuries. I guess that makes three reasons—but who's counting?

Without a soccer ball to stop him, I felt completely

helpless. The DJ was playing cheesy processional music as the princesses and their escorts started up the aisle from the back of the gym to the stage.

"Miss Eden Endicott," the DJ announced. Her black hair was piled high on top of her head in swirls and she wore a low-cut, slinky white dress. She was on the arm of Mark Jellick, the captain of the football team.

"Miss Sabrina Toth" was next. She wore her hair in a huge '60s-style flip and was on the arm of the co-captain of the football team.

"Miss Kiki Green" followed. She wore her hair long and straight and clung nervously to the arm of Pat Paceman, Aceman's older brother.

"Miss Alexa James," the DJ continued. Alexa's purple gown was so tight around the ankles, she tripped on her way up the aisle, but her boyfriend, the captain of the basketball team, managed to keep her upright—barely.

"Miss Robin Diehl" was in the spotlight next, followed by Desiree Washington, who must have modeled her hoop-skirt dress after Scarlett O'Hara's in *Gone With the Wind*.

"Miss Alison Cahill," the DJ announced. I didn't pay attention to what Alison was wearing. My eyes were on Boricius as he moved closer to the aisle.

"Egg will be fine," Colin said reassuringly. I was

clutching his arm and had probably cut off his circulation.

"Miss Eglantine Peabody," the DJ finally announced.

Well, she was beautiful, she was regal, and even Tino looked dignified. He probably would have fit right in back in Trewellyn. And Egg's authentic medieval gown caused quite a stir in the crowd.

Once all the princesses were settled on folding chairs decorated to look like thrones, the DJ presented last year's homecoming queen, now a high school student. Once she took her place, it was time to crown her successor.

I frantically checked out the crowd. "You haven't seen Ric, have you?" I asked Colin.

"He told me he wasn't coming," he answered.

So it was all going to happen the way I imagined it: Egg vanishing in front of the school . . . just to feed the ego of some ancient old magic hack.

"This is going to be bad," I whispered to Colin who looked at me as if I were crazy.

The DJ played some kind of fanfare–drum roll thing and then announced, "This year's Pine Glen homecoming queen is . . ."

Just as he stopped for a huge dramatic pause, which he must have practiced for days, a huge cloud of golden fog suddenly enveloped the stage, completely obliterating our view of the royal court.

"Great special effects," said Colin as the crowd around us admiringly clapped.

I closed my eyes for a moment, sure that when that smoke dissipated, Egg would be gone forever. Then I waited breathlessly as slowly the golden fog became a gentle haze, and the silhouettes of the princesses appeared. "She's gone," I murmured. "Egg's gone."

"What are you talking about? She's still there," Colin said.

Sure enough, *my* princess and all the other princesses were still sitting on their little throne-like chairs.

I quickly looked around for Boricius. I'd last seen him standing near the stage. Suddenly, one girl squealed and another and another. "A lizard! *Eeek!*"

In the spot where Boricius had last been seen was a bulgy-eyed lizard, slithering across the floor. And who was standing nearby, looking handsome, relaxed, and very pleased with himself? Ric. He bent over, picked up the lizard by the tail, and casually dropped it in his pocket.

"Calm down, everybody. It's just a lizard," the DJ nervously pronounced. His voice was a little shaky, considering he'd been totally unprepared for the evening's "special effects."

"This year's Pine Glen homecoming queen is Miss Eden Endicott!"

Eden acted surprised and managed to cry without messing up her makeup as last year's queen placed a rhinestone crown on her head. She then took her place on the throne of honor. But my eyes were on Egg, so beautiful, so regal, and still here in Pine Glen . . . at least for a little while. I looked back at Ric—but he was gone.

"Are you okay?" Colin asked.

I guess I wasn't exactly smiling. "I'll tell you a secret, if you promise not to tell."

Colin crossed his heart. "Promise."

"Egg is leaving tonight. For good."

I definitely caught Colin off guard. "Where's she going?"

"Back home," I said. "And she will never, ever be back."

Colin was plenty puzzled by that remark. "But why?"

"I can't explain that part. And she hasn't told Tino yet, so you can't say a word."

"I won't," he answered. He gazed up at the royal court on stage. "But things won't be the same around here without her."

I didn't want to cry on my first real date. "Let's dance," I said.

And that's just what we did, until the very last song had been played. I managed not to kick Colin even once.

❧✦❧

At 11:28, Colin and I slowly headed up the front walk of my house, hand in hand. I hoped that Egg and Tino were already home—his dad had picked them up. Colin's mom said she needed to drive around the block to pick up a quart of milk, and she'd be right back, but I think she was just giving us some privacy. As she drove away, I felt a little bit like my coach was about to turn into a pumpkin.

"I'm really sorry about your cousin," he said. "Are you going to be okay?"

"I'll be fine. And I had a really great time," I told him.

"Me too," he answered. "I still can't get over those special effects. Casey, Eden invited me to her Halloween party next Saturday night. Would you come with me?"

I was stunned. "Eden? At her house?"

"Yeah. We have to wear costumes."

My first thought was there's *no way* I'd fit in there. But then I thought of Egg, who assumed she belonged everywhere.

"I'd like to. I just have to ask my dad. Okay?"

"Great. I'll call you tomorrow." Colin gently took my chin in his hand and gave me a peck on the cheek.

My heart did a flip-flop. I'm almost positive he was about to zero in for a real kiss . . . but then a huge cloud of purple smoke wafted out along the sides of the front door.

"Casey—your house is on fire!"

"No . . . It just means it's time for me to go in. It's kind of a family joke," I tried to explain. The joke was on me, thanks to Ric.

Colin looked understandably perplexed as I dashed toward the door. It wasn't exactly the good-night I'd planned.

As I reached for the front doorknob, I looked back once more. "Thanks for everything," I called.

Colin waved in a dazed kind of way.

When I closed the door behind me, I was surprised to find Gran, Dad, and Shane sitting in the living room in their robes, waiting.

"Where's Ric?"

"He's in the den," Gran said.

Ric wasn't in the den, of course. It was Alaric, rummaging around in his velvet bag with frogs, toads, and lizards leaping everywhere. Duke was getting a workout trying to pounce on one, without success.

"Thanks a bunch, Ric!"

Alaric slowly turned toward me. The last time I'd seen him in his wizard getup, I thought he looked kind of silly. But this time, he looked just right. The pointed hat sat squarely on his head and it was as if he'd finally grown into his baggy robes. He stood very straight and looked supremely confident—even regal. I knew right away this was no apprentice. Alaric was a full wizard at last.

"Why do you look so surprised to see me, Casey?" he asked. "You knew I would come back, didn't you?"

"Your timing was less than magical."

Alaric nodded. "My timing? Ah, things did not go well with Colin?"

"It would have gone better if you hadn't used the front door. The purple smoke kind of distracted us."

"My apologies to you both." He sounded as if he meant it.

Duke rushed forward with a slithery lizard dangling from his mouth.

"Is that Boricius?" I asked.

"No, no," Alaric assured me. "He has returned to Trewellyn, I promise you."

I took the lizard, returned it to Alaric's backpack, and then shooed Duke away into the living room with the rest of the family. Alaric was still dithering around with his bag.

"I need to thank you for what you did for Egg

tonight. I guess you're a grand master now."

"Yes, even though it is not really acceptable to turn your teacher into a lizard. However, Boricius was not playing by the rules either, withholding information and not keeping his promises."

"I'm proud of you," I told him, looking directly into those emerald eyes of his. I sighed. "Are you and Egg really going to Trewellyn and never coming back?"

"I am afraid we are."

That wasn't what I wanted to hear. "Is she going to remember any of this? Like school or Tino or *us*?"

"Good question. I could erase it from her memory and she would not miss you. I could erase her from your memory, too. What do you think?"

I suddenly thought of Mom. "Remembering hurts. But forgetting hurts more," I said.

"How true," Alaric said. "You know, Casey, I think you would make a great wizard."

"I didn't think women could be wizards."

"Not back in my time and place. But here, in your world, yes, I think a female wizard would fit right in."

I shook my head. "No thanks. I'm not that crazy about magic."

"You mean nothing good came of it all?" Ric asked playfully.

"Sure, a few things. Like you introducing me to Colin—well, okay, you say that wasn't magic. But what about Carly's improved performance as keeper? And Heather's clutch goal?"

"Most of that was just . . . life."

"What about how you made Rachel Hanrahan move away?"

Alaric raised his arm as a postcard zoomed through the air and landed in his hand. "Before you make up your mind, please read what she wrote to her best friend."

I grabbed the card with lovely picture of the Alps on it.

> *Dear Sara,*
> *I can't believe I didn't want to move here—*
> *I was sure wrong about Switzerland. We*
> *live practically next door to a ski run and*
> *I've met the most gorgeous guy named*
> *Marcel! I've already made a ton of friends.*
> *I may never come back! Get your butt over*
> *here fast.*
>
> > *Lots o' love,*
> > *Rachel*

"Great," I said. "Why don't you get Sara's dad transferred there, too?"

"Casey, don't be mad at me." Ric stuck out his lower lip in a most appealing pout. "You know I'm going to miss you. And I'll always remember you."

"For another seven hundred years?"

"Way longer." Alaric reached out and gave me a big, brotherly hug. I inhaled deeply to take in a large whiff of cinnamon and ginger. *Yummy.*

Tears burned my eyes. "Is there a spell to keep me from crying?"

"Yeah. But you don't want that." He let go and his green eyes grew dark. "Why don't you see if the princess is ready."

I reluctantly headed toward the bedroom. "Send me a postcard sometime, Ric, okay?"

When I turned back, he was gone.

"Casey, can you help me?" Egg asked as I entered our room. "Alaric forbade me from bringing anything back to Trewellyn but I must take these with me." She held out three pictures. One of the whole family that Dad had taken with the timer on the camera, a picture of Egg in her cheerleading outfit and me in my soccer jersey, and a shot of Egg and Tino at homecoming.

"I thought we could sort of tie them on my leg. This long skirt will hide them."

I found some of her ribbon streamers. While I was tying the photos, she asked me a question.

"Tino shed a lot of tears at our farewell. 'Tis it all right for a football player to cry?"

"Yeah. As long as the rest of the team didn't see him." I knotted the ribbons, then tucked the photos in. "You know, Coach Curson is going to be real disappointed you're not running track in the spring."

"I know." She sighed. "Perhaps I shall try a couple of laps around the jousting yard now and then. If only I could instruct the royal shoemaker to make running shoes."

I made one last tug on the ribbons. "There you go."

"I wish I could take a phone," she said.

"Me too. Colin invited me to a Halloween party at Eden's house next week and I'd love to tell you all about it."

The princess moaned and fluffed out her full skirt. "Oh, I can hardly bear to miss it! That Colin is quite besotted with you."

"Yeah. I don't know exactly why," I admitted.

"He likes you for who you are. Because you like sports and don't squeal and dress frilly. Did he kiss you good night?"

"Sort of," I said, feeling shy. "Ric kind of ruined it."

She moaned again and straightened her tiara.

"Alaric, Ric . . . I wonder if he can really get me back to Trewellyn after all. But I must try. I suppose I am ready. Ready as I'll ever be."

Egg took a deep breath, lifted her head high and walked out of the room. I followed her like a puppy dog . . . like Duke . . . like a lady-in-waiting. After all, she was my princess.

Alaric stood in the middle of the living room, surrounded by the family. Dad, Shane, and Gran looked as if they couldn't quite believe what was happening. Egg solemnly took her place next to the wizard and addressed us as if we were all her royal courtiers. At least we'd moved up from being peasants.

"Kind Peabodys, you have been most loving to me, a complete stranger. My heart shall be with you always. But I am a princess and 'tis my duty to assist my father, the king, and to govern when he no longer can. So on this night of homecoming, I must bid ye farewell."

"We understand," Dad mumbled.

"Of course," Gran said. "But, my dear, we will miss you so much!" Her voice cracked. I felt pretty shaky myself.

Shane rushed to the princess's side and surprisingly threw his arms around her waist. "Don't go!" he pleaded.

"You know I must return to my castle," Egg said gently.

"Then take me with you!" he implored her.

"Shane, come on, you're making it worse." Dad gently led him back to the couch.

Duke rushed forward, yipping and wagging his tail. "Duke!" she said, bending over to pet him. "We shall be home anon!"

"Alaric!" Gran's tone was sharp. "You promised us Duke would stay."

"Worry not, fair lady," the wizard said, bowing.

"Alaric! You promised me Duke would be with me in Trewellyn when I arrive," said the princess.

"Ye need not worry, Your Highness. Now, for the farewells. First, let me say that I thank you all for your generous hospitality to the princess and myself. And the cuisine was exquisite." He bowed to Gran. "We are eternally grateful."

"It was our pleasure," Gran said. "Right?"

We all nodded in agreement. I thought I caught a few tears welling up in Alaric's eyes. Then he turned toward the princess. "Your Highness?"

"Part of me shall always be a Peabody," Egg said. "Yet, should something happen to my father, only I could carry on in his place. Thus with a heavy heart, I leave you."

She walked over to Dad, who seemed to be in a daze, threw her arms around him, and gave him a huge hug. "You are the king of this castle and a very fine king, indeed."

"I'll miss you," he said in a husky voice. "Try not to throw too many people in the dungeon."

Next, Egg approached Gran for a tender hug and a kiss on each cheek. "I always wanted a grandmother and now I have one. You are the kindest person I have ever known."

Gran didn't even pretend not to cry. "I love you, princess. Remember that."

Shane came next. For an eleven-year-old who usually avoids hugs, he sure knew what to do. "My cousin Shane. How I wish I could take you with me. For of all the Peabodys, you would most enjoy Trewellyn."

"I got an A on my juggling speech," he told her in a shaky voice.

"Of course you did."

"I'll miss you," Shane whispered.

"Me too," she whispered back. "Think of me when you play Battle Royal."

The princess turned to me. "My cousin Casey. I shall miss you the most, for you have taught me the most."

"What?" I asked, totally caught off guard.

"How to run, how to share, how to stand up for myself. You even taught me that the earth is round. Aye, I believe it now. I shall always remember you."

As we hugged, Egg thrust something in the palm of my hand and closed my fingers around it.

Duke stood next to me, wagging. The princess bent down and kissed the top of his shaggy head. "I shall see you anon, in Trewellyn, Duke."

She returned to the center of the room and held her head high, looking most royal.

"I am ready, Alaric."

Alaric cleared his throat. "I hope somebody has the . . . um . . . box?"

"Oh yeah!" Dad reached behind a sofa cushion and pulled out the ancient, rusty box that had started it all.

Alaric took it, then reached in his bag, pulled out a vial of shiny powder and sprinkled some inside the box. He pulled out his wand, tapped the box, and began to mutter, "Aldus, baldus, ruckus, roe . . ." The box began to glow.

Alaric tossed some of the powder on the princess and the chanting became louder. "Pransus, dansus, discus, doe . . ."

"Farewell," said the princess. "Farewell, dear Peabodys." She waved to us. We waved back.

Alaric was practically shouting now. "Domicus, homicus, gravus . . . go!"

With that, he tapped the princess on the shoulder with the wand. Duke began to whine as a thick cloud of golden fog enveloped her.

"Farewell . . . ," she said, her voice growing fainter.

All at once, she was gone, but the box in Alaric's hand glowed brightly. "Farewell," said the wizard, waving his wand.

There was a puff of purple smoke and when the vapor dissolved away, the princess and the wizard were gone. For once, Alaric had gotten the spell right and I might never forgive him for it! All that was left was the box, and a lone frog hopping on the ground. Duke chased it around the room.

"Well, at least he left us the box," Shane said. "And Duke's still here!"

"We always knew *our* Duke wasn't *her* duke," Dad said.

"I know, but she almost had me believing he was," I admitted.

"Don't, Duke! That's mine," Shane said. He managed to catch the frog with both hands. "I can keep him, can't I, Dad? I'll call him Wizzie, short for grand master wizard."

Dad almost seemed pleased. "Sure. We'll get a tank for him tomorrow."

Gran had some tissues handy and passed them around.

"I feel like I just woke up from a weird dream," Dad said.

"I know," Gran agreed. "I don't think I'll ever be the same."

I suddenly remembered I had something in my hand. I unfolded my fingers and there was a single pink pearl earring. Princess Eglantine Eleanor Annalisa Ambrosia de Bercy of the Kingdom of Trewellyn had given me one of her mother's earrings and kept one for herself. We would always need each other to make a perfect pair.

22.

Ye Ever After

My room seemed deserted without Egg in it, but surprisingly I fell right to sleep, clutching one pearl earring in my hand. Maybe Alaric had put some kind of sleeping spell on me. Or maybe it was all that dancing.

The ringing phone woke me up early the next morning. It was Tino, hoping he could catch Egg before she left, so I had to give him the bad news.

"She said I can't write or call or anything. What's up with that?"

"She's going to a really strict boarding school." It wasn't such a big lie. "I'm sorry, Tino. I'm going to miss her like crazy, too."

I thought I heard sniffling as he mumbled a quick good-bye.

When Alisha came over later, we kicked my soccer ball around and I told her as much as I could about Egg going home. She couldn't believe she'd left in such a hurry.

"Don't tell me we have to go through cheerleading tryouts again!" she said. "Nobody can replace Egg."

On Monday, the whole school was buzzing when everyone found out Egg was gone. Even the teachers seemed to miss her, and Coach Curson was outright mad to lose a potential runner. Egg's presence was still felt, though. Half the girls at Pine Glen wore ribbons around their legs or streamers in their hair.

No ribbons for me—they're not my style. But I pulled my hair back in the chunky barrette with the glittery stones that the princess had left behind, and I proudly wore her Doc Martens. Colin thought I looked "chilly." I didn't look like a princess, but I looked like *me*.

Not everybody missed the princess, of course. Maddy could barely hide her delight at her rival's sudden departure. She followed Tino around like a puppy again, but he didn't even seem to notice her.

On Tuesday, the *Pine Glen Gazette* came out with some awesome photos of Egg as a homecoming princess, and on Wednesday, it was announced that Maddy would be her replacement on the cheerleading squad. She'd had the second highest score after the princess, but everybody knew it wasn't close at all.

Somehow I got through the week. We had an away soccer game on Thursday and a few guys came to cheer. That was nice, but the big shock was that Desiree Washington and—surprise—Kiki Green, showed up, too. (I'm not sure Eden would approve.) They were pretty enthusiastic, though they didn't sound quite the same without Ric or Egg leading them. I scored one goal, Alisha scored two, and near the end of the game, I passed to Lindsey and she scored her first goal of the season. She even thanked me afterward. I guess I'd become a team player at last.

Colin and I spent a lot of time trying to figure out what to wear for Eden's Halloween party. I suggested he go as a wizard, figuring I could give him some tips, and I decided to be a witch. Gran scoped out second-hand stores to find props and costumes.

Dad and Shane concentrated on taking care of Wizzie. They set up an elaborate tank and got a stack of books from the library about frogs. It was a great distraction, but I could tell they missed our princess.

Of all the Peabodys, though, Duke seemed to

suffer the most. He moped around and occasionally whined for no good reason—especially when he stared up at the metal box on our coffee table. Gran had polished it until it glowed.

On Saturday, we beat Columbia at soccer and Alisha won her first MVP award. I got high praise from Coach for assisting on all three of Alisha's goals. When I got home, I showered and was thinking about getting ready for the Halloween party. That's when I heard Duke whimpering. By the time I got to the living room, he was barking and running in circles around the coffee table.

Dad, Gran, and Shane rushed in after me.

"Quiet, Duke!" Dad yelled, but he just kept on whining and barking.

"What on earth is the matter with him?" Gran asked.

Duke suddenly stopped and raised a front paw. All the fuss seemed to be about the box that had brought us our princess.

"Should I open it?" Dad asked.

"Yeah, Dad. Now," Shane insisted.

"Just be careful, dear," Gran warned him.

As before, Dad grunted and pulled and pushed and twisted, but this time he didn't need to pry the box open with a screwdriver. He gripped one corner and the whole thing began to shake wildly.

"It's her! It's the princess!" Shane shouted.

"What if it's something worse?" Dad asked. "Like a . . ."

Just then the box shimmied right out of his hand and dropped to the floor with a thud. The lid flew open and a brilliant golden fog filled the air.

"Egg?" I called out. "Is it you?"

"Casey!" a voice replied faintly.

Duke ran around, barking. Shane hopped in a circle like a four-year-old. And when the fog drifted away, there she was—Princess Eglantine Eleanor Annalisa Ambrosia de Bercy of the Kingdom of Trewellyn, in her beautiful gown, her glittering tiara, and one pink pearl earring.

We screamed and hugged and screamed and hugged some more. Duke got a squeeze, as well.

"Oh, Duke, when I saw you in Trewellyn, I was worried that you would not return with me!" she told him. He wagged his tail.

Finally we calmed down enough to sit in the den and hear Egg's story. We had a million questions.

"How did you return?"

"Where's Alaric?"

"How was your father, the king?"

"Can you stay?"

The princess was regally patient waiting for us to calm down, and then she began her story. "Alaric will not be coming, I'm afraid. But I'm planning to stay as long as you will have me."

"Which is *forever*," Gran said. No one disagreed.

"Thank you, Gran. I returned home to Trewellyn expecting a royal welcome. Instead, the place was turned upside down! It seems that right after I left, my father went off to war. He arrived in Coothwaite and discovered that his enemy, King Prisby, had died, leaving behind a widow, Queen Devona, and a daughter, Princess Idella. Father was tired of warring, and Queen Devona was still young enough to bear a son, so he married her and brought her and Idella back to Trewellyn!

"When I arrived, Princess Idella was being waited upon by *my* lady-in-waiting, and the queen was about to give birth to a son, or so my father hopes. If she does, he will be the future king of Trewellyn. I will no longer be first in line for the throne!"

"Oh no, that's terrible," I said.

"It *was* terrible. Idella threw a fit and refused to share her chamber—*my* chamber—with me. Zounds—she was quite rude about it!"

I flashed back to Egg's first night in my room, and smiled.

"Where two princesses dwell, there dwells trouble. That's what Father always says," Egg gloomily recalled.

"Didn't your dad miss you?" Shane asked.

The princess dabbed at her eyes with a handkerchief. "Oh, Shane, 'twas most upsetting. Apparently, in Coothwaite, my father's mind became muddled with love or some such emotion. 'Twas like he barely knew me. Like I was just some peasant girl come in to scrub the drawbridge."

"What did Alaric say?" I asked.

"He believes the queen's own wizard put a curse on my father, else he'd have been most joyful to see me. Even worse, Queen Devona treats Alaric as her personal servant, leaving him little time for his important work. Really, I wish he'd turn her into a dragon—'twould not be such a stretch, you know."

"But weren't you supposed to go back to the exact moment you left?" Shane asked. "Isn't that how time travel works?"

"Well, you know Alaric," the princess mused. "He's always a bit off in his spells. Though I'm not sure he didn't do this on purpose, to show me my future."

I thought of Ric, his sense of humor, and his amazing green eyes. Egg was probably right.

"Then there was Prince Vorland, mooning around the castle grounds, absolutely useless. I told Alaric to concoct a love potion between him and Princess Idella and be rid of them both. And do you know what Alaric said?"

We all leaned in to hear the answer. "He said, 'I don't think they'll need a potion'! Can you imagine that wretch liking Idella more than me?"

Of course, we couldn't.

"But he did." She turned to the dog. "And you, Duke, you saw it all. If only you could tell them."

Our dog obligingly woofed.

"Are you ever going back again?" Gran asked.

"Alaric says that I may visit again. He's trying to develop a counterspell right now. However, he believes I shall be safer here with you for now. Oh, 'tis so good to be home!" Egg settled back on the couch, kicked off her royal slippers with the gold buckles, and smiled.

But there was no time to relax! "Call Tino. You've got to go to Eden's Halloween party with us," I told her. "Everybody's going to flip when they see you!"

"How is Tino?" The princess seemed genuinely concerned.

"Terrible. He's not going to the party, even though Maddy's been trying to persuade him."

That was all Egg needed to hear. She rushed off to call Tino, and I hurried to our room to look for another costume.

I could hear Dad and Gran talking in the hallway.

"Looks like everything's back to normal," Dad said.

"Normal for the princess and the Peabodys." Gran laughed.

After we made a few calls, Tino and Colin arrived together to pick us up for the party.

Gran had the guys' wizard costumes all arranged. At the last minute, she'd turned my witch's black cape into a wizard's black robe and fashioned an extra pointed hat for Tino. It made me a little lonesome for someone else.

While Egg was getting ready with the help of Gran—her new lady-in-waiting—I opened my bedroom curtains and gazed up at the night sky. There was a full moon—perfect for Halloween.

"Ric, if you're out there somewhere," I said to the stars, "thank you. Thank you so much!"

That night, the princess wore my full Panthers soccer-team attire: jersey, shorts, long socks, even cleats. Her hair, in a ponytail, poked through my favorite baseball cap. I wore her gown of pink satin with billowing blue brocade sleeves, trimmed in gold braid, and her glittering tiara, twinkling with diamonds, rubies, emeralds, and sapphires.

No one seemed to notice that each of us wore one pink pearl earring.